JUST LIKE MARTIN

OSSIE DAVIS
JUST LIKE MARTIN

SIMON & SCHUSTER BOOKS FOR YOUNG READERS

Published by Simon & Schuster

New York • London • Toronto • Sydney • Tokyo • Singapore

SIMON & SCHUSTER BOOKS FOR YOUNG READERS
Simon & Schuster Building, Rockefeller Center
1230 Avenue of the Americas, New York, New York 10020
Copyright © 1992 by Ossie Davis. All rights reserved including the right
of reproduction in whole or in part in any form. SIMON & SCHUSTER BOOKS
FOR YOUNG READERS is a trademark of Simon & Schuster.
Designed by Lucille Chomowicz
Manufactured in the United States of America
10 9 8 7 6 5 4 3 2 1

Library of Congress Cataloging-in-Publication Data
Davis, Ossie. Just like Martin / by Ossie Davis.   p.   cm. Summary:
Following the deaths of two classmates in a bomb explosion at his Ala-
bama church, fourteen-year-old Stone organizes a children's march for
civil rights in the autumn of 1963. [1. Civil rights movements—
Fiction.   2. Afro-Americans—Fiction.   3. United States—History—
1961—1969—Fiction.]   I. Title.   PZ7.D2974Ju   1992
[Fic]—dc20 91—46725 CIP
ISBN:0–671–73202–1

To all the grandchildren on earth,
including Ruby's and mine

1

"You're going to get it!" With all that noise in the kitchen, she had to stoop down, lean across, and put her face almost in mine to make herself heard. "Reverend Cable is mad as the devil at you, and he wants to see you right away!"

It was Dorasthena, my best friend—the prettiest girl I know, but sometimes, the meanest—looking as if to say I told you so. "I wouldn't be surprised if he didn't break your neck."

"Wants to see me about what?"

"About PeeWee. I told you not to bring him in here, that he was going to mess up, but you wouldn't listen, would you?"

"PeeWee? . . . what's he done this time?" I was on my

knees peeling Irish potatoes in a washtub for the potato salad the sisters were making in the church kitchen, together with the fried chicken and the homemade pound cake and sweet potato pies baking in the oven. Dorasthena knew that busy as I was and with all I still had to do, I didn't have time for no—any—foolishness. But she plowed right ahead as if whatever it was she was yapping about was bound to be my fault.

"Them television reporters asked Reverend Cable about it. He hit the ceiling."

"Asked him about what?"

"About PeeWee."

"PeeWee?"

"He's in the office, getting himself cussed out. You better get in there before Reverend Cable commits murder on that fool."

I whipped off the apron I had borrowed, wiped my face and my hands, dropped my knife, and started out the door. PeeWee! Ever since I had asked him to come to the church to help me out with the march he hadn't been nothing—anything—but trouble.

"And where do you think you're going, Isaac Stone?" Big Mother was standing over a pot of boiling water. She had flour on her hands up to her elbows from making pie crust. Two other sisters were in the kitchen also: one mixing cake batter in a great big bowl, the other at the sink washing pots and pans. Big

Mother was built like a Mack truck—voice and all.

"To the pastor's office."

"I don't need you in the pastor's office, I need you here, peeling them Irish potatoes. You, too, Dorasthena, somebody's got to pluck these chickens. And somebody's got to gut them and wash them and cut up the parts and dip them in my batter so they can be fried. And where is Hookie Fenster and Billy Cabelle and Mollie Mae Sanford and Carole Ellery? More than a hundred people going up to the march from this church alone, and I got to feed 'em all. I need help, but not a deacon in sight, nor young folks neither. Don't let me have to report you-all to Reverend Cable."

Nobody knowed—nobody knew—how old Big Mother was. But once she got started everybody got out of her way. Lucky for me one of the big pots full of potatoes boiled over. "Lawd, have mercy!" she shouted as she ran back to the stove.

"This is an emergency, Big Mother," I shouted, grabbing Dorasthena by the hand and dashing out into the hall.

Downstairs at Holy Oak Baptist used to be big and spacey, with a storeroom, a rest room, a furnace room, the church kitchen, and a little chapel with benches and a blackboard where the Young People's Bible Class met every Sunday. And a recreation room down at the other end. But now, since Reverend Cable was helping to organize the March on Washington, which had been set for Wednesday, August 28, 1963, everywhere you looked was chock-full of something or other: boxes, crates, pamphlets, posters, picket signs—all stuff we needed for the march, which was only two days away. He had turned over the main office upstairs to Mrs. Rhettis, the church secretary, while he had taken the downstairs storeroom, put in a phone and a desk, and made it into his headquarters with me as his helper. It was here that he spent most of his time, and that's where we were headed now.

The basement was crowded: people coming and going, children scrambling all over, everybody excited, like the March on Washington was the biggest holiday black people was ever gonna have. Some bringing food: cakes and pies, crates of live chickens. One man was dragging a suckling pig. Some bringing supplies or carrying messages. Some with cameras and tape recorders. Reporters and photographers all over the place talking to people and snapping pictures. A television crew from Germany was hanging around in the rec room, where Hookie Fenster and Billy Cabelle were sure to be hiding out waiting to see the pastor. We had to push our way through.

"I told you 'bout PeeWee, when you first brought him in here. But you wouldn't listen."

"No cause for you to be jealous, Dorasthena."

"Jealous? Me? Of somebody ain't no bigger than a minute! I told you wasn't no use trying to civilize that idiot. Reverend Cable put you in charge, not him; but ever since they had you on television, shaking hands with Martin Luther King, Jr., you think you a saint. You don't have to listen to nobody."

Dorasthena always bosses people around, but she didn't mean no harm—any harm. It's just the way she is if she really likes you. And she was right as usual. I was Junior Assistant Pastor, as well as president of the Young People's Bible Class. And everybody in it—including PeeWee—was my responsibility. Reverend Cable had said one more stupid trick from PeeWee—like stealing a barbecued chicken and giving it to the television crew, or wandering into the ladies' room by "mistake"—like he did last week, and he'd be out on his butt. And I didn't want that to happen

The door was shut when we got to Reverend Cable's office, which was unusual. And some people were lined up outside or sitting on the benches watching and waiting. It worried me that everything was so quiet. Not a sound was coming from inside.

"I thought you said Reverend Cable was hitting the ceiling?"

"Maybe he killed him already." Dorasthena whispered.

We knocked twice, then opened the door and went in. Reverend Cable was sitting at his desk with his back to the door. Usually he talks very loud to people on the phone, but now he was listening quietly. So I figured it must be Dr. King he was talking to. PeeWee stood in front of the desk, his big eyes wide open, twisting his cap in his hand, grinning, with that wide gap between his two front teeth, which everybody knows is the sign of a born liar. The more innocent he pretended, the guiltier he looked. Always.

"I tell you, Martin, this march is the biggest thing ever happened to this town, especially for black folks. More and more people signing up every day. We've already decided to rent a separate bus just for the young people. All right, I'm leaving tonight. The buses will leave tomorrow morning. Say hello to Coretta and the children, and I'll see you in Washington."

He hung up, swung around, looked straight at me, then grabbed some of the papers spread out on the desk and started signing. I could tell he was mad—was angry: "Stone"—most people call me by my family name—"didn't I tell you that none of you children was supposed to talk to these television people without my permission?"

"Yes, Reverend Cable. I told everybody exactly what you said."

"Then how is it that when I got here just now I find PeeWee Higginbottom standing outside my office, grinning into the television cameras, and telling the whole wide world that he was captain of the youth bus?"

"I only said that because Stone isn't going to the

march, and he's appointed me to take his place." Pee-Wee grinned, looking for me and Dorasthena to back him up.

"What do mean Stone isn't going? What's to keep him from it? He's captain of the youth bus—aren't you, Stone?"

"Yes, sir. Just like you appointed me to be, sir. But Daddy said—"All of a sudden I was completely out of words. I felt ashamed for not having told him earlier. But I kept putting it off, hoping against hope.

He laid down the papers and looked at me. "Your daddy said what?"

"He said I couldn't go."

"Not go to the March on Washington! Is Isaac out of his mind?"

"'Too far away for a boy his age,' he said. 'It would be too dangerous.'" This from Dorasthena, my best friend, butting into my business.

"And besides, he doesn't believe in non-violence—or you, and Dr. Martin Luther King, Jr.—he doesn't believe in anybody." This from PeeWee, as much as I had tried to do for him.

"All right, all right, that's enough. I'm talking to Stone. Is it true, Stone, that Ike won't let you go to the March on Washington?"

"Yes, sir, it's true, sir. But maybe if you would ask him one more time—"

"I've already asked him more than one more time. I

even sent him a note—by you—asking him to call me, telling him how important this is, begging him to let you go. Did you give him my note?"

"Yes, sir. He read it. But said he didn't want me that far away from home."

"And then he took your note, sir, and tore it up." Dorasthena again. Tell her something in strict confidence and look what happens.

"But I need you, Stone. You're Junior Assistant Pastor of this church—president of the Young People's Bible Class. What am I going to do without you?"

"I'll do it, sir," said PeeWee. "I'll be glad to be in charge—bus captain, all the way there and back."

"PeeWee, I'm going to tell you this for one last time: Stone is head of the Young People's Bible Class here at Holy Oak, my Junior Assistant Pastor, not you. The only reason you're here is because Stone begged me. He wants you here. Is that clear?"

"Yes, sir, but I was just saying, if Stone can't go, send PeeWee. Ask Stone himself, he'll tell you how good I am, sir."

"I already know how good you are, PeeWee, and that's the trouble. The next time you shove your face into somebody's television camera and start running your mouth, I'm going to strangle you with my bare hands. Now get out of here."

"Yes, Reverend Cable, sir. But Stone can vouch for me. As a matter of fact he wants me to take his place. If you don't believe it, ask him."

"Out, PeeWee. Back to the kitchen, if Big Mother will have you. If not, go home." He pushed PeeWee out and closed the door behind him.

"Stone, why on earth did you pick a dummy like Pee-Wee to be your assistant, instead of Hookie Fenster, or Billy, or some of the others?"

"He could have picked me."

"PeeWee is an orphan, sir. He needs a chance," I said, ignoring Dorasthena.

"Of course, PeeWee is an orphan, that's his profession, and boy is he good. You should have heard what he was telling them television people about how lonely his life was. I would have cried too, if I didn't know better. PeeWee is also an idiot and a troublemaker—just like I told you. But I'm not talking about him, I'm talking about you. Three full buses from Holy Oak set to roll at five o'clock tomorrow morning. Why is it that I had to find out from PeeWee that you can't go? Why didn't you tell me yourself?"

"Well, sir, I was going to tell you, but you've been so busy."

"Too busy to talk to you? You know better than that."

"Then, first thing this morning, Big Mother met me at the door and pulled me into the kitchen to peel potatoes."

"He was afraid, that's why he didn't tell you." Dorasthena again.

"I wasn't afraid. I just thought that, maybe, after he

thought about it some more, Daddy would change his mind."

"Change his mind? When did Ike Stone ever change his mind about anything? Where is he now?"

"He's home. He's working nights this week. Probably asleep."

"Call him. Wake him up. I need to talk to that thick-headed father of yours."

I grabbed the phone and dialed, let it ring. It took him a while to grunt and wake up. "Daddy," I said, "It's Reverend Cable. He wants to talk to you—"

Reverend Cable grabbed the phone and shouted into it, "What in God's name is the matter with you? Have you gone crazy? This is the March on Washington. Don't you know what that means? . . . Nonsense, man, quit acting like a fool! . . . I have tried to reach you. I sent you a note, asked you to call me. No word from you. I need Stone. I need all the help I can get, and Stone needs this march, Ike. This is very important, especially for young black people. This is history. And I'm— Ike . . . Ike . . . Well I'll be . . . " He caught himself in time to keep from cursing. He shook the phone then slammed the receiver down. "Can you beat that? Can you beat that! He hung up in my face! Hung up in my face. You two get in the car!"

Reverend Cable's car was big enough, but as always the backseat was loaded, this time with books and posters and picket signs and banners and flyers for the march. An old football helmet and a cardboard box full of secondhand clothes for the poor were on the floor. So the three of us climbed into the front. Dorasthena scrunched up in the middle, hugging her knees. Everything seemed strange and quiet as we went flying along the streets. It was hot and sticky like August always is, and nobody much was out. The radio was off. Nobody felt like talking—I know I didn't—not just now. I just sat staring straight ahead and thinking about my daddy.

I love my daddy most when he is mean and ugly, with danger in his eyes, and won't say a word to nobody, 'cause that's when Mama Lucy said he needs love most. According to her, Ike Stone was bound to hurt somebody one of these days if he wasn't careful. He needed watching over, which was why she hated so much to have to die and leave him and me by ourselves. Not that he was a bad man, she kept reminding me. He had come back from the war wound up too tight. And now that she was dying it was up to me. He would need somebody to understand him. Stick by him no matter what. Listen to him even if he didn't talk. Which mostly he didn't. Somebody to cook his meals, see that he ate right, wash his clothes, sew buttons on his shirt. Most of which she taught me to do before she died.

Reverend Cable—as Daddy's oldest buddy—was supposed to watch out too, but his patience was short.

And after Mama Lucy died, he soon gave up. So by now probably the only real friend my daddy had left was me.

I remember one night in particular, me doing homework at the table, her in the rocking chair, darning his socks, and him sitting in the corner, his head hung down, not moving. Not saying a word. Until finally she jumped up, threw the sock down, and came and stood in front of him. "Ike," she said, "whatever happened to you over there in Korea? Whatever it was, you'd better talk about it. Get it out of your system once and for all, else it's gonna drive you crazy."

Ike looked up almost as if Mama Lucy had slapped him. I'd never heard her talk like that to him before.

"Stone is your son. You got to set him a better example than sitting here all the time like a corpse. I ain't gonna be with you-all always, and life must go on. Your son needs talking to and listening to and so do I."

Ike jumped up too. "Shut up, Lucy, you hear me? You just shut up. I'll call your name when I want to hear from you. Until that time you just keep your mouth shut!"

He was a foot taller than she was, but she looked him dead in the eye. "Go ahead, Ike, hit me. Kill me, if killing somebody'll make you feel any better." Ike stumbled back like lightning had struck him. "Go ahead. Hop into your truck like you always do, and leave us here alone. Go. Anything, rather than stay in this house another night with a ghost like you!"

He tried to speak but I don't think he could. He choked, and stared at Mama Lucy like a crazy man. He stumbled out, slamming the door behind him, jumped into his old pickup truck which was parked under the chinaberry tree out in the backyard, and went roaring off.

I expected her to run out and try to stop him like I seen—I saw—her do one time before. But she didn't. She smiled at me, sat back down as if nothing had happened, picked up the sock, and started in where she had left off.

I waited as long as I could, but then I had to speak. "Mama Lucy—"

"Son"— she cut me off, pretending to laugh as she talked—"your father wasn't always like that. At high school, where I first knew him, he was as different as night and day. A football-playing fool." She turned her face away and dropped her eyes, then came back to herself, smiling. "I wasn't too bad myself: ninety-five pounds wringing wet, but I knew how to fit my skirt and middy blouse. I was real tight with Cable at the time—he wasn't a preacher then. No, Lord. Cable was a big time rascal—especially with the girls. But not your father—he was always quiet and shy. Cable was the quarterback, Isaac the end. Boy, could he carry that ball! And I was the cheerleader. Oh, they were real good buddies; went to college together, to Howard University. Ike stayed on campus one week, then got on the train and come back home, and we got married.

"Later, he and Cable went to the war together, come back together, but then it was different. Something happened over there made Cable a preacher, and your father . . . well you can see for yourself. Oh, Ike was the sweetest, gentlest, kindest thing you ever saw when we was first courting. But after the war, after he came back home . . ." She took a little handkerchief from her pocket, which had a very nice smell to it, and patted her eyes. ". . . And now it's time for you to go to bed."

I scrubbed my teeth, put on my pajamas, and came back to the living room to kiss her good night; but she wasn't there. She was in the sewing room, her room, the smallest in the house, where she kept a closetful of sweet smelling dresses, all of which she had made with her own hands. The door was closed, but I could hear the whirring of the old Singer sewing machine that was her pride and joy. That was always her way when she was worried—locking herself in and making a pretty dress even if it took all night. And hanging them in the closet. Some she had never worn. So I didn't bother her. I went back to my room, said my prayers, and got into bed.

Reverend Cable parked in the front yard and we got out and came up on the porch. Daddy was sitting there with a dirty old towel spread across his knees with his pistol on it. His pistol! On the floor between his feet was a rag, a box of cartridges, a brush with small round bristles, and a can of gun oil. I was completely surprised: Daddy was cleaning his pistol, right out there on the front porch for all the world to see! Reverend Cable didn't bat an eye. He acted as if he didn't see what Daddy had in his hand.

"Ike, I want to talk to you."

"Go ahead, preacher, talk. It's what you always do." Daddy held up his blue steel Smith & Wesson .38 revolver to the light and squinted through the barrel. "But I think I ought to warn you: Everybody ain't non-violent, like you and your Reverend Dr. Martin Luther King, Jr., and I want these folks 'round here to know that."

"Ike Stone . . ."

"I especially want these kids to know it." Daddy looked down at me and Dorasthena. "Somebody come after them, like Buford Leggitt, the Edlee brothers, or Bull Connors, they got somebody to back them up, ready to shoot back—not put his tail between his legs like a dog, not turn the other cheek—you kids remember that. Hand me that oil can, will you Dorasthena?"

Dorasthena looked first at Daddy, then at Reverend Cable. She reached for the can, but Reverend Cable stopped her.

"Stone, would you and Dorasthena leave Ike and me alone for a little while?"

I didn't want to leave. I wanted to stay, but Mama

Lucy had taught me to always be polite, and obedient to my elders. "Yes, sir." I took Dorasthena and went into the garage, which was built right next to the house. I got my toolbox, put it up on a table, and started to open it. But Dorasthena shushed me. "Be still," she said, putting her ear to the wall. "I want to hear this." So I decided to listen too.

"Ike." Reverend Cable was trying real hard to control himself. "You're trying to provoke me. Sitting out here where everybody can see you, making a fool of yourself. Put that thing away!"

"I'm a man, Josh Cable, not a child. I don't turn the other cheek, so watch how you talk to me!"

"Whatever you say to me, or do to me, however outrageous, I'm not going to let you provoke me. I promised Lucy that."

"Of course not. You're too much of a Christian. White man walk up, spit in your face, you tell him how much you love him, right?"

"You know me better than that."

"White man is serious; he's out here to kill you, or put you back in chains, and you out here singing and praying, begging for rights the white man's had for a thousand years; demonstrating, marching on Washington . . . out here playing games."

"Games? You think hundreds of thousands of black people, from every walk of life all over this country, standing at the Lincoln Memorial in the sight of God and all mankind, petitioning for their rights, their freedom, is playing games?"

"One thing, I ain't letting no son of mine go to Washington. He's staying right here with me. Now if you will excuse me—"

"I will not excuse you. You can play with that pistol all you want, but I'm here to talk to you, and that's what I intend to do."

"So talk. I got some night work over at Simmy Creek bridge, so I ain't got all day."

"Let him go, Isaac. It'll be good for him. Be good for you too. You ought to come along and be there yourself. I mean how long you gonna go on like you been, all bottled up inside yourself? Come on, Ike, spit it out, let it go. Come on. Get on the bus. You can ride with Stone and PeeWee and the rest of the young folks. Give yourself a chance to be young again, come on."

"You don't want me up in Washington, preacher. I ain't a religious man, like you."

"You used to be. You and I were raised up together in Holy Oak Baptist. You courted Lucy there, you married her there, I was your best man."

"I got no faith in the white man, and, if God is white, that goes for him too!"

"Isaac Stone, that's blasphemy!"

"I promised Lucy to look after the boy, see that nothing happened to him. And that promise I intend to keep, come hell or high water! Somebody hurt my son,

I'd have to go up there and find him, and kill him, blow Washington, D.C., clean off the map! Now you wouldn't want a crime like that on your conscience, would you, preacher? No, sir. Only way I march on Washington is at the head of an army infantry division, like in Korea."

"Korea was bad enough, and then for God to turn right around and take Lucy after you got back was almost too much for one man to bear. I can understand that, but—"

"What happened in Korea is over and done with, and as for me, and Lucy and God—it's none of your business. And now I've got to go."

He came off the porch and into the backyard where he found Dorasthena and me pretending to work on the tree house. "Don't wait up for me, boy. They stopped the traffic so we could work on the bridge. It'll probably take all night." He climbed into the truck, put the pistol into the glove compartment, and drove away.

Reverend Cable stood and looked after Daddy a long time. It was easy to see how tired he was. Then he got back into his car and just sat there, with his shoulders sagging, and his head bowed down.

I wanted to show Dorasthena the tree house I was building with my toolbox, but Reverend Cable said we didn't have time, so I locked the front door and climbed back into the car. Dorasthena didn't have the common decency not to talk about my private business right in front of Reverend Cable. "I think your daddy ought to see a doctor."

"See a doctor for what?"

"Because he's crazy."

"Dorasthena, how can you say a thing like that?" I looked at Reverend Cable but couldn't tell if he was listening to her run her big mouth.

"Sitting there, on the porch in broad daylight, with a gun in his hand—that's crazy. I think your daddy should be put away."

I was so mad—so angry at her—I shut my mouth and clenched my teeth to save what was left of my temper. I mean, when it comes to fathers, Dorasthena Foster of all people is the last person in the whole wide world who should talk!

2

The churchyard was a crazy house, boiling over with people, jostling in the morning dark, laughing, reminding each other not to forget the straw hats, shoes for walking, and the suntan lotion, yelling to be heard above the noise of the three buses which all had their motors running and their headlights on. Leaving-time from Holy Oak Baptist Church was 5:00 A.M. sharp, and Reverend Cable was a stickler for being punctual. Anyone not on board would be left behind. Nobody wanted to miss the March on Washington.

I was in the middle of helping the men load the last containers of cans and bottles packed around with ice onto the baggage bins with the rest of the food and choir robes and posters and placards and flyers, when Mollie Mae Sanford and Carole Ellery found me. You'd almost think they were sisters, but they weren't. Just close friends, always together, and dressed much too pretty, and expensive, for a march. Everybody said they were too young to wear perfume, but they did it anyway.

"Stone, Stone"—Mollie Mae sounded like a lady in distress—"PeeWee and Hookie Fenster are arguing over who is captain of our youth bus. They say that you're not going?"

"That's right, Mollie Mae, I'm sorry, but Daddy won't let me."

"Won't let you? But why? This is the March on Washington! This is Negro history." That was Carole, as you might expect, so ladylike and proper, just like Mollie Mae.

"I know, Carole, but don't you think you two ought to get back on the bus? It's almost time to leave."

"Oh, here you are—the two of you." It was PeeWee who came running up waving a great big flashlight. "Tell them, Stone, tell them."

"Tell them what?"

"That I'm the one in charge since you're not going. And you better tell Hookie Fenster too. We leave in seven minutes," he said, looking at somebody's watch he'd borrowed. He turned and started back to the buses.

"PeeWee, we are talking to Stone, not you." Mollie Mae shouted after him.

"Yes, so just shut up!" Carole chimed in. But PeeWee had already disappeared into the dark.

"But why, Stone, why won't he let you go? I think that's awful."

"Yes, Stone, you're president of the class. How can we go without you?"

"Daddy, well, he just don't believe—he doesn't believe—in marching and picketing and demonstrating and Martin Luther King, Jr. He thinks the march is silly. But don't worry, everything is going to be all right."

"You don't have to listen to your father, if he's going to be that mean."

"Oh, yes I do, Carole. Anyway, my daddy is not mean. He just doesn't understand things yet, but he will. Everything is going to be all right. Please, Mollie Mae. Please, Carole. Go and get back on the bus."

"First Dorasthena, and now you."

"What do you mean, first Dorasthena?"

"We don't know where Dorasthena is."

"She hasn't showed up yet, and it's almost time to go."

I wasn't exactly speaking to Dorasthena, not after what she had said about Daddy. Still I had looked for her in the sanctuary when everybody went to hear the send-off speeches. All the seats were taken. Reverend

Cable had already gone, so Mrs. Rhettis led us in prayer, then spoke to us about what a big moment this was going to be in Negro history, something we could tell our children's children. Then Mr. Mac McIllister, the oldest black lawyer in Alabama, got up and said the exact same thing. Then Deacon Guiness led us in prayer again. Everybody knew his prayer would be too long. Mrs. Ellis was all over the place, pinning flowers on people, and Big Mother started handing out lunch boxes even before the deacon was finished. Dorasthena had to be there somewhere—probably hiding, I said to myself, so we would miss her and see how important she was. But she'd show up with some outrageous excuse. She wasn't about to miss the March on Washington. That, I knew for sure.

PeeWee came running up again, waving the flashlight. "Hey Mollie Mae, hey Carole, get a move on. You're holding up the bus."

"Aw, shut up, PeeWee, ain't nobody talking to you."

"Oh, yes, you are, Mollie Mae. I am captain of our bus, and either you do be talking to me, or you ain't going."

"You ain't captain of the bus—no such thing. Stone is."

"I am so the captain. I'm saying it's time for all aboard—and that's for both of you. Else we're gonna pull off and leave you. Right, Stone?"

"Right, PeeWee. Look, Carole and Mollie Mae, I'm

still the president, even if I can't make it this time; but we can't let personal feelings get in the way."

"I'm going to see Reverend Cable."

"Me too."

"Reverend Cable's not here. He's already up in Washington."

"Then I'll talk to Mrs. Rhettis."

"And I will too."

Mollie Mae and Carole started off. I ran and caught them. "Mrs. Rhettis's got a million things to do, and we members of the Young People's Bible class are supposed to help, not run around bothering people. Reverend Cable is counting on us to do our part. And I'm counting on it too. PeeWee will do just fine."

"PeeWee's not the only one, it's Hookie Fenster."

"Him and Billy Cabelle and Roscoe Malone—already they're starting to sound like cats and dogs," Carole said.

I was beginning to worry about Dorasthena, but being president I thought it best to put Mollie Mae and Carole back on the bus myself—a little personal attention, which they liked a lot of—before I went inside to look for her.

The bus was full. Not only us, but young folks from other churches had been invited, and already it was like a party: Pearlicia had her guitar and was sitting in the backseat playing and singing along with some others; Hookie Fenster and Roscoe Malone were horsing around as usual; Billy Cabelle was working on his camera; and everybody talking so loud you could hardly hear yourself. I had to push my way up the aisle and down again.

"Anybody seen Dorasthena?"

Nobody answered or even paid any attention. Some of the kids had already opened their lunch boxes. "You know Dorasthena—probably won't show up till the very last minute," PeeWee shouted.

"I'd better go take a look around." I started off, but Hookie stuck his foot out, and I stumbled over it and fell. Hookie and Roscoe thought that was very funny.

"Come on, Stone," PeeWee said, helping me up. "Quit playing around." As if I had tripped myself. "It's time for us to go."

I looked at Hookie as hard as he looked at me, but decided to keep my temper. "One more minute, Pee-Wee, she's got to be around here somewhere." I jumped off the bus, but Hookie jumped off right behind me and grabbed my arm.

"I'm sorry you're not going, Stone, 'cause you and me, we got some unfinished business." Ever since Hookie found out that I was trying to be nonviolent, like Dr. King, he'd been trying to make me break my vow. "And as for PeeWee, he'd better stay out of my way. Else I'll give him a taste of what I been saving for you." He balled up his fist and shoved it under my nose. I slapped it away as hard as I could and stared at him.

"Hey, hold it, buddy. I thought you were supposed to turn the other cheek. No? . . . Good. We'll see how hard you can slap as soon as I'm back from Washington." He grinned and got back on the bus.

I couldn't for the life of me imagine where Dorasthena could be, so I ran all over the church, upstairs and down, calling her name. But she was nowhere to be found. I got to the upstairs office just as Mrs. Rhettis was coming out.

"Mrs. Rhettis, have you seen Dorasthena anywhere?"

"No, Stone, I haven't. Isn't she on the bus?"

"No, ma'm. Nobody seems to have seen her. Mind if I use the phone?"

"Go right ahead, but we're already late—and lock the door behind you." She looked at her watch and hurried out.

I went inside and dialed Dorasthena's number. But a voice came on and said the phone had been disconnected. Again? I thought as I hung up and ran back outside, getting there just in time to see the last bus heading out into the streets and around the corner. One second later a little piece of daylight squirted out from behind the steeple. They were starting late. Reverend Cable wouldn't like that at all. They were going without me. But even so, it still felt good just standing there watching them leave.

I stayed around the church and helped Mr. Fenster

and some of the church sisters clean up the mess and put things back in order. Big Mother sent me downstairs to see about Reverend Cable's office. There wasn't too much I could do; big piles of papers and books and things cluttered his desk. He has his own special way of knowing where everything is and forbids anybody to touch what's already there. I finally decided it would be better just to leave everything exactly the way I had found it.

I swept the floor and emptied the trash, then Big Mother called me and I went into the kitchen and sat down with Mr. Fenster and Deacon Ashley. Big Mother gave us all the grits and bacon and eggs and ham and sausage we could eat.

The sun was up and climbing when I left the church, and though there was a little bitty breeze left over from last night, I could see it was going to be another hot and sticky day. Daddy had worked all night on the Simmy Street bridge and would probably be back home by now and sound asleep. I started to catch the bus, but changed my mind. I was still worried about Dorasthena, so I decided to walk the mile or so from the church to her house over on Burden Street.

"Probably half way to Chattanooga by now," I said to myself, thinking about the buses, and the good time everybody must be having, and how I already missed being with them, and not being at the March on Washington taking place tomorrow. Reverend Cable had said he wanted us to meet all of the Civil Rights leaders and shake their hands. Here I was a thousand miles away, walking by myself through the quiet and empty morning. I crossed the railroad tracks and took a shortcut through the freight yard, where two or three empty boxcars were standing on a siding. It made me think about hopping freight trains, like Daddy and Reverend Cable and Professor Duckett used to do when they were boys. That's how they first went to college—hitching rides and hopping freight trains. Someday maybe I would get to do everything they did, the way they did it.

I also thought about my argument with Dorasthena: "Sitting out on the porch, polishing his pistol right in front of the whole wide world. What is he, some sort of gun nut, or something?"

"Naw, my daddy ain't no gun nut. He bought it for protection, that's all."

"Protection from what?"

"Well, when Daddy got back from the war they gave him a pretty good job in the foundry. But one day, this fellow, one of the Edlee brothers—you know about the Edlee brothers?"

"Everybody knows about the Edlee brothers. They hate colored people."

"One of 'em was working there, and he called Daddy a nigger. Daddy took an ax handle and put that sucker in the hospital. If it hadn't been for Mr. Mac McIllister, Daddy would probably still be in jail. He told the judge he had witnesses to prove that it was five against one. My daddy beat them all, but it was in self defense. The judge gave Daddy a suspended sentence, otherwise he might still be doing time. I was just a baby, but Mama Lucy told me about it."

"Stone . . ."

"Yeah?"

"If that had been you they called a nigger instead of your father, what would you have did?"

"Have done."

"You always got to correct everybody, got to be so proper."

"You got to speak right if you want to go to college. And anyway—"

"Would you have been nonviolent, like Dr. King say? Would you turn the other cheek somebody call you out of your name like that?"

"Of course I would."

"Suppose somebody was to hit you—just walk right up and slam you in the face, would you do it then?"

"Well, that's what Dr. King said; that's what Jesus said."

"But you ain't no Dr. King, and you sure God ain't no Jesus. You can get mad like everybody else. I seen you. Just like your daddy. And Hookie Fenster says that you're a liar and a hypocrite."

"I am not studying about Hookie or anybody else. I made a vow and I intend to stick to it. But like I was saying, they fired Daddy, but the Edlees swore that one day they was gonna—they were going to—hunt Daddy down and kill him. So Daddy went and bought himself that pistol. But Mama Lucy wouldn't let him keep it in the house. He had to keep it outside in the garage, in the glove compartment of his old truck, which he still does."

"Even so, I still think your daddy—and his pistol—should be put away somewhere for safekeeping." I saw then it was no good trying to talk to Dorasthena, so I gave up.

The house on Burden Street was old. It sat back from the street and sagged a little and needed a coat of paint. Sort of run down, it was, like the rest of the neighborhood. The grass needed cutting, the little hedge was scraggly, and nobody seemed to pay much attention to the flowers. Dorasthena's mother had died when she was born. She had a picture of her in a little gold locket she showed me once. Her grandmother had run the house, but now she was dead, leaving Dorasthena to look after everything by herself. I would never say this to Dorasthena, but I was a much better housekeeper than she was. Mama Lucy had seen to that. Daddy had built our house himself, as a wedding present to Mama Lucy. Even though she was dead, he and I kept that place spic and span, shining like new money. People still talked about it. Best-looking house in the neighborhood, some of them said.

Dorasthena never invited any of us to her house. Her father was a drinking man, with strict rules against her hanging around with boys, so I hadn't been here in a long time. There was a sign in the yard that said BEWARE OF DOG, although they hadn't had a dog since I can remember. Daddy had told me to stay away from Rufus Foster, and so I did, mostly, up till now. Dorasthena had had her heart set on making the trip to Washington with the rest of the class. Mollie Mae and Carole had even bought her a special blouse just for the trip. She wouldn't have missed it for the world. Something had to be wrong; so I went up on the porch and knocked at the door.

There was no answer for the longest time. So I knocked again. And then again. Finally the door opened just a crack. "Who is it?"

"It's me, Dorasthena. I thought maybe—" Before I could finish she slammed the door in my face. But not before I had seen the big black ugly bruises on her cheek and under both her eyes. I almost cried, coming down off the porch.

I felt sorry for Dorasthena but I wouldn't say that to her face for anything in the world. Her father had been a good man before he took to drinking, and now every once in a while he beat her. Once he gave her a black eye and she tried to cover it with powder. But everybody knew, especially Mrs. Edison, her homeroom teacher, who didn't have any children of her own. Dorasthena was her favorite. Mrs. Edison had gone to Reverend Cable more than once, and together they had spoken to Mr. Foster, who always cried and said he was sorry and wouldn't do it again. They told him that if he raised his hand to Dorasthena one more time that they would go to the courts and take her away and turn her over to Mrs. Edison, who loved her like a mother and would be glad to give her a home. But Dorasthena was like me, she had a special affection for her father. She always asked them to give him another chance and promised to tell them if it happened again. But she never did. And this time she wouldn't either. I know Dorasthena. But it certainly made me angry. It's a good thing for Mr. Foster that I am so nonviolent.

I can tell sometimes just by the way he does things that Daddy wants to talk, but he doesn't know how to get started. Usually I just wait, but this day was different. The March on Washington was taking place, and I wasn't there, and I couldn't for the life of me think of anything else. He finished breakfast, and we sat awhile saying nothing, but he wanted to talk. I could tell.

"Good coffee, son, good coffee, just like your mother used to make me."

"Thanks, Daddy." And that was that. He couldn't seem to think of anything more, and I was too busy waiting for him to leave so I could turn on the television. But he didn't leave, he stayed. He even helped me clean up the kitchen, and that was a surprise.

Then he said: "How about you and me driving way out to the lake and catching us a few perch for supper?"

Now, God knows I don't like hunting. I feel about shotguns and rifles and all that stuff just like Mama Lucy— I don't like 'em! I was glad Daddy didn't keep his pistol in the house. But fishing? That's different.

I always fixed us a good picnic basket while Daddy got the fishing gear together. Then we'd drive up to the lake, rent one of Mr. Peterson's old leaky boats, and row way out. Just Daddy and me, the two of us together, not even talking if we didn't want to. It was something, putting the worm, live and squirming, onto the hook, throwing it as far out into the water as you can, then just sitting there, slapping mosquitoes, and waiting for something to come along and bite. You'd see the cork starting to bobble, and then go under. You'd jerk the line to make sure, then pull him on in, and let him flop around in the bottom of the boat. Nothing in this world I like better than fishing with Daddy.

But this was March on Washington Day. All I did was to thank my daddy very much, but tell him, no— not if he didn't mind.

"This is one of the biggest things ever happened to black folks in this country. I'd like to watch as much as I can—on television. If you don't mind?"

"Well, all right. If that's the way you want it." He got

his hat and fiddled with it awhile. And then he said, "I've got a few runs I can make, I guess, one over to the brick yard. If Uncle Phil, or Oscar, or Vern, or any of the rest of 'em should call, say that I ought to be back before five." He got to the door, then spoke again: "Phil called me last night; wants you and me to leave Alabama, go live with him in California." He laughed, but it didn't sound funny.

He wasn't out of the door good before I turned on the television and there it was, the March on Washington! It was almost as if I was there myself.

In one shot I saw what must have been hundreds of buses pulling into their parking spaces. Thousands of people, as far as the eye could see, gathering from all over the country at the Washington Monument. There was music, and people singing songs, some of the words I could hear, and important people I could recognize, talking to the crowd on microphones. And then the crowd turned and started marching along beside that big long silver pool of water toward the Lincoln Memorial, sitting there high and white and almost holy. I listened to all the speeches, but I was too busy trying to spot Reverend Cable and the people from Holy Oak to pay much attention, until Dr. King started to speak.

I jumped up, ran to the phone, and tried to call Dorasthena to make sure she was listening too. But I'd forgotten—thanks to Rufus Foster—the phone was disconnected. Her television would probably be in the pawnshop.

So I sat down, as close to the set as I could get. Dr. King's voice was clear and electric, like it was straight from the pulpit, and aiming straight at me—like good preaching, only better, and stronger, something you wished would never stop.

"*Now* is the time," he said, "to make real the promises of democracy. *Now* is the time to rise from the dark and desolate valley of segregation to the sunlit path of racial justice. . . . *Now* is the time to lift our nation from the quicksands of racial injustice to the solid rock of brotherhood. *Now* is the time . . ." That one sentence over and over, and each time he said it, the whole crowd would be lifted higher and higher, right along with him—me too—like we were a part of the music in his voice.

And then he started in about the dream he had.

"I have a dream," he said, "that one day this nation will rise up and live out the true meaning of its creed: 'We hold these truths to be self-evident; that all men are created equal.'" I remembered that from Thomas Jefferson in Mrs. Morse's history class.

"I have a dream that one day on the red hills of Georgia the sons of former slaves and the sons of former slaveowners will be able to sit down together at the table of brotherhood.

"I have a dream that my four little children will one

day live in a nation where they will not be judged by the color of their skin but the content of their character.

"I have a dream today."

Something about those words, and the way he was saying them, made it hard to stay in my seat.

". . . So let freedom ring from the prodigious hilltops of New Hampshire. Let freedom ring from the mighty mountains of New York. . . .

"Let freedom ring from every hill and molehill of Mississippi. From every mountainside, let freedom ring."

Big words, strong words, beating at me like a hammer. I never had such a feeling in all my life! ". . . All of God's children, black men and white men, Jews and Gentiles, Protestants and Catholics, will be able to join hands and sing in the words of the old Negro spiritual, 'Free at last! Free at last! Thank God Almighty, we are free at last!'" By the time he finished I found myself standing—I don't know how—in a chair, jumping up and down, yelling and laughing and clapping. Like I had run through the television and was there right in the middle of the crowd. Right next to Dr. King himself! No idea of time or space or what my own name was, until Daddy's hand reached up and touched me on the shoulder.

I tried to tell him, to describe it to him—like having wings and sitting on hot air rising; like being on top of everything there ever was and looking down . . . big bright light exploding in the pit of your stomach; quoting to him the words that I remembered, exactly the way Dr. King himself had said them. Powerful words . . . magical words. Daddy waited till I was finally able to stop myself, then went to the television and turned it off.

I felt a little guilty, but I couldn't help myself. Something strange and wonderful had happened to me, and I had left him out. He looked at me. Gave me a minute to cool down, then, "How about you and me going out to the cemetery this afternoon, huh, carry Lucy some flowers?"

Cemetery visits we usually do every Sunday on our way back from church. I think of it as special because, truth to tell, that's when I feel that we are still a family: me, Daddy, and Mama Lucy, together again. But this wasn't Sunday. This was Wednesday, the day of the March on Washington. "Flower shop's closed, Daddy. Mrs. Ellis is gone, along with everybody else. I saw her get on the bus."

Ike went to the window and looked out. And then he started for the door. "Let's go anyway, spend some time with your mother."

The heat had died down some by the time we got there. Out on the hillside it was calm and green and peaceful; a little breeze fanned up, like a visitor in from the river. The city noises seldom reached this far, and were more like a hum from somewhere out of sight and in the distance.

We parked near the bus stop, went inside the gate, and walked till we came to the family plot. Mama Lucy was on one side, with space left for Daddy, and for me. With a nice shiny headstone that had her name carved on one side and a place for his on the other. He took a bag from his pocket and offered it to me. "Some boiled peanuts?"

"Thanks. Don't mind if I do." Boiled peanuts were his favorite. Mine too.

We looked awhile at Mama Lucy's marble slab, which was clean and neat. Ours was the best kept plot out there. We always put the peanut shells back into the bag. He sat beside me on the grass, leaned back on his elbows, and talked. "You wanted to go to Washington a whole lot, didn't you?"

"Yes, sir. More than anything."

"And you think the reason I said no is because I am mean?"

"No, sir. . . . Well, maybe you are mean, in a way; but Reverend Cable said he thought it was about Korea, and stuff." I know he didn't like for anybody to mention that word, so I stopped.

"Maybe you think I was jealous because you spend more time with Josh Cable than you do with me?"

"Well, sir, I don't exactly know what to think."

"I don't mind. He's your godfather. That's the way Lucy wanted it. But . . . well, you see, boy, since Lucy's gone, you're all I got left. If I was to lose you—"

"Lose me?"

He thought about what he was trying to say for a long time before he continued. "There's this dream, this awful dream I been having here of late: We in this dark, dark place, you and me and your mama; we're lost and it's getting darker. And it's hard to breathe, almost like asthma, and us trying to find the way out. But there isn't any. Suddenly a big flash of lightning and thunder blows us all apart, and splinters and plaster raining all over our head, and gun smoke—that's what it smells like. It's like I'm almost blind and I can't find you-all. But I can hear Lucy, she's trying to find you, too, and calling your name and screaming at me, begging me to do something. But the deeper I dig down into this red hot rubble, the farther you get till I can barely hear you. I reach out to grab you, but I keep missing, son, I just keep missing!"

We sat there awhile, with him looking at me in the funniest kind of way and shaking his head. He wiped the sweat from his brow, then looked away again.

"I mean, if something was to happen to you, if God was to take you from me, like he already took Lucy . . . I miss her, son. God knows I miss that woman. . . . Sometimes I go into that room of hers with the sewing machine . . . and I open the closet and look at all them pretty dresses she always made, some she never even wore . . . but I can't look long. I have to close the door to keep from crying. I—I wonder what she would say about me not letting you go."

He got up, turned his back, and looked out over the

river and toward the hills. "Maybe I should have gone with you, but I didn't . . . I couldn't. I can't go back to church; I tried, but I can't. But I know she still wants you to go. And that's why, even though God and me ain't back on speaking terms, I keep up her membership, I pay her dues. And every Sunday I drive you all the way across town to Holy Oak, then sit outside in the parking lot and wait till you finish. And then I drive you home. Right?"

"Right."

"You're a good boy, Stone. I love you, even if I don't always show it. Lucy would be very proud of you; you're smart, get good marks, and I'm saving up every month to send you to college."

"Morehouse. I want to go to Morehouse." I said. I wanted to make sure that he was clear about that.

"I know, I know. Morehouse College, 'cause that's where Dr. King went. Right?"

"Yes, sir, and that's where I want to go."

"Well, I promise you one thing. I'm sorry for the way I behaved about Washington. And I want you to forgive me for that. Now I can't be nonviolent, but I do promise that, from now on, whatever you do, about Dr. King, and marching—and all that—I'm not going to stand in your way. You understand what I'm saying?"

"I understand."

"Good!" he said, sounding much relieved. "Hey. How about you and me, just the two of us, go over to

Roselle's for a plate of barbecue and beans and cole slaw?"

"Roselle's closed. I saw her getting on the bus this morning with everybody else. She's gone too."

Just then a long, slow freight train whistle echoed across the valley. I could still see the trestle where the railroad tracks crossed the river, but just barely. Back of that, stretched out in a long low line, were the hills, dark and rolling, and night was just beginning to move in this direction.

"You want some more peanuts?" he said, offering me the bag. I took the last handful, as we stood together and watched until finally all we could see was the fading taillight on the caboose.

3

The first Sunday of the month is always Youth Day at Holy Oak, and I was one of the junior ushers supposed to work in the sanctuary at the eleven o'clock service. But I had already missed Sunday School, which takes place at nine o'clock, because this was the day before Labor Day, and Daddy had to work later than usual. The drive across town to Holy Oak only took about fifteen minutes, and we would have made it, except the right rear tire blew out. Daddy got out to fix it. I had on my white usher's suit so I couldn't do much to help. By the time we pulled in and found a place in the parking lot the service had already started. Daddy gave me money, both to put in the collection and to pay Mama Lucy's dues, and I went in.

Dorasthena was waiting for me at the side door. One

eye was still a little puffed, but I didn't mention it.

"Reverend Cable and Mrs. Rhettis been looking all over for you, Stone. He even started late 'cause you weren't here." Dorasthena didn't mean to, but she always sounded like she was blaming people.

"Daddy had a flat."

"I know it don't mean nothing to you, but your friend PeeWee's taken over. He's ushering all over the place. And showing pictures."

"What pictures?" I asked.

"That Billy Cabelle took of him and all the others up at the march."

The church was packed, every seat taken. This was the first Sunday after the march, and naturally everybody was excited, whispering back and forth to each other, even in the middle of the service. Latecomers were standing around against the back wall, so Hookie Fenster, Billy Cabelle, and I went down into the basement to get some folding chairs from the furnace room, which is where we had to stack them after Reverend Cable had taken the storeroom and made it into his basement office.

"Stone, man, y-y-you should have been there." That was Billy Cabelle, who stutters when he gets excited. "Yeah, man. And PeeWee, he was something else." That was Hookie. "But you ought to heard what he was saying about you: called you a phony and a hypocrite and a liar."

One of the real reasons I was so close to PeeWee was

that Hookie was against it. It got to be a contest to see which one of us was better for PeeWee to have for a friend. Naturally, Hookie kept trying to stir up trouble between us. So, instead of answering I smiled in his face, put a chair under each arm, and went back up stairs to the sanctuary.

PeeWee, looking very satisfied with himself, was acting as junior head usher—my usual job—handing out bulletins and fans and hymn books, then leading people down the aisle and finding them seats. He looked at me and winked. I didn't wink back. This was church and church is supposed to be sacred.

"Look at Mollie Mae and Carole—aren't they beautiful?" Dorasthena came up to me and whispered with a big smile on her face. It was true. The two girls, who were ushers also, were dressed in white; but not in the uniforms the other girl ushers wore. Their mothers had hired Mrs. Ellis, who did sewing as well as selling flowers, to make them something special.

"I thought you weren't speaking to those two?"

"Oh, Stone, you so dumb. You don't understand nothing about people. Of course, I'm speaking to them. They're my friends, ain't they?—aren't they?"

I found out later that Mollie Mae and Carole had not only bought Dorasthena a blouse to go to the march in the first place, but had also brought her back a brand-new beautiful silk scarf. I was not surprised. We all grumbled about Mollie Mae and Carole, mostly because their parents had the money to give them anything they wanted. They always stuck together, and sometimes they could really get on your nerves. But nobody at school or in the Bible class could beat them giving: always buying you a present or something when you least expected it, lending people money if they needed it, and never asking to get it back. Wasn't a mean bone in their bodies. Nobody could stay angry with Mollie Mae and Carole for more than a minute or two—it just wasn't worth it.

The gospel choir was singing "Blowing in the Wind," which they had sung on the steps of the Lincoln Memorial, louder and prouder than I had ever heard them before. And when they finished everybody in the church stood up and applauded, something I had never seen before in a church service. Then Reverend Cable, wearing his brand-new black and red robe that made him look at least another foot taller, rose from his seat, stepped into the pulpit, stood there, and looked out at the congregation, not saying a word. The place got so quiet you could hear a pin drop. People even stopped fanning.

"Children," he finally said, in that big, deep voice of his, "I am so happy—so grateful to God Almighty that he has let me live to see this day—that I could cry."

"Go ahead, Reverend, cry if you want to," somebody said, and everybody else said "Amen."

"Everybody was there. Over two hundred thousand people, black and white, North and South, marching, marching, marching. Roy Wilkins, from the NAACP, was there. A. Phillip Randolph, from the AFL-CIO, was there. Dorothy Height, National Council of Negro Women, was there. Jim Farmer stayed in jail in Plaquemine, Louisiana, but his spirit was there. John Henry Lewis, from SNCC, was there. Jews were there. Catholics and Protestants were there. People from colleges and labor unions were there. And somebody even told me that Malcolm X was there. Hallelujah! And great God Almighty! Martin Luther King, Jr., was there.

"But I don't have to tell you about it. Those of you who couldn't make it, couldn't have missed it if you tried. It was all over the television they tell me. Bull Connors couldn't have missed it. Governor Wallace, standing in the doorway of the University of Alabama, he couldn't have missed it. Senator Eastland, from Sunflower County Mississippi, home of the White Citizens Council—he couldn't have missed it. The dastardly coward who hid in the bushes and shot Medgar Evers in the back in Jackson, Mississippi—he certainly couldn't have missed it. The Ku Klux Klan, they couldn't have missed it. The Edlee brothers, they couldn't have missed it. The high and mighty men who run this town, they couldn't have missed it."

By now the amens, the hallelujahs, the foot stomping, and the hand clapping were so loud we could hardly hear the words, but that didn't matter, we already knew the meaning ahead of time.

"The March on Washington for jobs and freedom

has focused the eyes and ears of the world, for the first time since the Civil War, on black people. And we now have a golden opportunity to strike such a blow for freedom as we have never struck before. So what I want to talk about this morning, what Martin Luther King told me to come home and ask you this morning is this: Are we going to stop now?"

Everybody in the church shouted "No!"—me the loudest of all.

"This is the time and this is the place," Reverend Cable said, with tears rolling down his face, "to let the whole world know, that what they saw in the March on Washington, Great Glory! that was a small skimption. When it comes to marching and picketing and demonstrating and sitting in and singing and praying and going to jail and, yes, even dying for our freedom, they ain't seen nothing yet!"

Once again, the entire church rose to its feet and applauded. People stomping their feet and shouting, throwing their hands up into the air, yelling at the top of their voices, hugging each other, and crying. Me too. I never saw anything like it in my life.

When service was over, I said good-bye to Dorasthena, who was riding home with Pearlicia, then went to see Reverend Cable in his study, where he was dictating a telegram.

"Dorasthena said you wanted to see me, sir?"

"And get those off right away." He finished with

Mrs. Rhettis and then he turned to me. "Missed you, Stone, you and Dorasthena, at the march. Missed you a lot."

"And we missed being there. How did it go, sir? Was PeeWee all right?"

"Worked like a charm. I can't understand it . . . had those kids in line every step of the way. They were eating out of his hands. You yourself couldn't have done better."

"PeeWee's okay, Reverend Cable. He just needs somebody to believe in him, and have patience with him, that's all."

"Well, patience with PeeWee is something I haven't got. But, thank God, you do. I spoke to Martin about you."

It took me a moment before I could answer. This was a big surprise. "You did, sir?"

"He still remembers how helpful you were, you and Dorasthena, when we had that march downtown earlier this year, before he went to jail. He sent you this." He handed me some paper with typewriting on it. "It's a copy of his I Have a Dream speech. I asked him to autograph it for you."

"Oh, thank you, sir. I heard it on television." I couldn't sit still . . . I took the pages and held them in my hands like they were Mama Lucy's best chinaware.

"Martin always had a special thing in his heart for young people. He thinks the time has come . . ." He stopped, got up from his desk, and stood for a while, looking at the wall. I was twitching all over. I couldn't wait to get somewhere and read those precious words aloud; but Reverend Cable had something else on his mind.

"Time has come for what, sir?"

"As I said in my sermon, Martin's planning a major campaign: marches, demonstrations, sit-ins, whatever it takes, right here in this city, right after the schools are open. And he wants to involve you children."

"You mean, let us march too? Along with the grown-ups?"

"Yes, yes, but some of us think having children in the line of march would be too dangerous. What do you think?"

Dangerous? I thought it was the most exciting thing I'd ever heard. "But, sir," I reminded him, "you had children march in the March on Washington."

"Washington is different. In Washington we had complete protection. But this is Alabama. You remember how it was earlier this year when we first demonstrated downtown. You were there. They cursed us, they spit on us, they threw stones at us. And then, the police, instead of protecting us, they started in too. Water hoses and police dogs. Swinging at our heads with billy clubs. It was terrible. And yet, in spite of it all, not one of us raised our voices, just kept on singing, remember?"

"Oh, yes, sir, I remember."

"That's what nonviolence means. But I was scared to death, not for us grown-ups, but for you children. That's when I decided that from here on in, we'd keep the children out of it. I still feel that way. But Martin disagrees. He says that this is a struggle involving all the people, children included. He wants us to train the children, teach them how to protect themselves but still be nonviolent, then let them march with the grown-ups."

"We did it the first time, last April, sir. And none of us got hurt," I reminded him.

"But that was only a few of you. Martin is talking about every kid in grade school. Everybody. You think, if we did let some of the older ones march, that you children would have enough discipline, enough self-control, to be nonviolent too?"

"Oh, yes, sir." This was sounding better all the time. Just wait till I tell Dorasthena, I thought.

"You see, if we had gotten angry and lost our temper and struck back, even in self defense, that would have caused a race riot, right there in the streets. Some of us, and maybe some of them, would have gotten hurt, maybe even killed. A thing like that could set the cause of freedom back for years to come. So, no matter what they did to us, we had to hold our tempers, keep our self-control. We had to show them, to prove to the world, that they might hate us, but we don't hate them.

We come in love, we come in peace, marching, not for vengeance, but for justice. That's what nonviolence is: the only way to make them see us, not as the enemy, but for what we really are, just human beings like them. You understand?"

"Yes sir," I knew all the answers, and could hardly hold myself together. "Because we are Christians, not supposed to hate your enemy, but to love them—and if they smite us, to turn the other cheek, like it says in the Bible, right, sir?"

"Well, yes, that's what it's based on; but there's more to it than religion, or being a Christian. It's got some Br'er Rabbit in it too—the only practical way I know by which people who are weak can confront the mighty and the powerful, and sometimes even over-come them. Like Mahatma Gandhi did against the British in India. You understand?"

"Oh, yes, sir. I understand." Reverend Cable had preached it more than once. How Mahatma Gandhi, way across the world in India, had led his people to freedom, how he taught them to be nonviolent, and how they followed him and refused to fight. And how the British had many soldiers in India, but couldn't use them. And finally got so frustrated, they left and went home. I knew all that; but I was thinking about how wonderful Dr. King looked making that speech. "I Have a Dream." I couldn't get it out of my mind.

"Of course you do, Stone. It's not you I'm worried

about, but what about the others? PeeWee, Dorasthena, Mollie Mae, Carole, Hookie Fenster, Billy
Cabelle, Pearlicia—your classmates? And others your
age from all over the county. You think that you and I
could make them understand what nonviolence is?
How it works? You think they would learn it . . .
how to use it . . . if we taught them about discipline,
and self control, how to protect yourself out there in
those streets but not strike back? I was thinking . . .
maybe if we set up a workshop . . . creative nonviolence for children, right here in Holy Oak. What do
you think of that?"

"Workshop?" I'd never heard that word before.

"Classes, every Saturday afternoon, right here in the
church. Just like we have in Sunday School—for children. You think they'd come?"

"I would."

"I know you would. It's not you I'm worried about.
You're my Junior Assistant Pastor. I can always depend
on you, but what about the others?"

"Oh, yes, sir. I'm sure they would," I said, but still
thinking about how those wonderful words would
sound coming out of my mouth! "I have a dream
today." I still remembered exactly how he said it.

Reverend Cable walked from one side of the room to
the other, then back again. "I'm still not sure about it,
not sure at all, but I said we would. So this is what I
want you to do. Tomorrow is Labor Day, and on
Wednesday you kids go back to school. Right?"

"Yes, sir."

"Talk to them, Stone, the children, sound them out. Tell them about the workshop, see how many might be interested in coming. Okay?"

"Yes, sir, and thank you for bringing me the speech. And sir, do you think Dr. King would mind if I committed it to memory, and sometimes recited it, like in the school assembly for Negro History Week — if Professor Duckett lets me?"

"I'm sure he wouldn't, but why not write Dr. King and ask him that yourself?"

"Oh, thank you, sir. I'll go home and do that right now." I started to dash out; he stopped me at the door.

"Stone, this is not child's play. This is serious business. There's a whole lot of hatred out there in this city. People who'll stop at nothing to keep us down."

"Yes, sir, but we're not going to let them keep us down, are we, Reverend Cable? That's what Dr. King's speech is all about, isn't it? For us to get our rights like everybody else. And that's why I intend to learn it by heart just as fast as I can."

He looked at me, smiled, and patted my shoulder. "Like I said: if it were me, if I had to give my life the way Medgar Evers did, then so be it. But if, God forbid, something were to happen to one of you children . . . Still, if that's what Martin wants . . . and, Stone—" He stopped, and sighed. "When you get on your knees to say your prayers tonight, pray for me too. Pray for Martin, for all us grown-ups. Tell God we're trying to do the best we can. Come on. I know Ike's waiting. I'll walk you to the door."

On the way home Daddy and I stopped by Mrs. Ellis, who made dresses, and sold flowers, too, real and homemade. Also she dealt in real estate on the side. Gladiolus were always Mama Lucy's favorites, so that's what we always bought. Mrs. Ellis was a lady who never stopped talking, especially where Daddy was concerned: about his health, and my future, and how we were getting along without a woman in the house. Daddy called her a hypocrite, and said all she wanted was a chance to get her hands on Mama Lucy's beautiful, unworn dresses, hanging in the sewing room closet, which Daddy swore nobody would ever touch. So he always sent me in to get the flowers, while he waited outside.

And Mrs. Ellis was still pretty, I suppose you could call it that, although she wore a wig, and Dorasthena called her dumpy. She was a widow and had been looking for a husband ever since she had moved here from Montgomery. And when Mama Lucy died, I think she sort of set her sights on Daddy. He made it his business not to pay any attention to Mrs. Ellis, or any of the other sisters who kept smiling up at him. Just flowers—mostly gladiolus, once a month, or sometimes twice— that was all Mrs. Ellis could do for him.

She had the flowers all wrapped and ready. As usual,

she was full of questions—why hadn't I gone to the March on Washington with the rest of the young people from Holy Oak? Was I ready with enough clean clothes—especially underwear—to go back to school, come Wednesday? How was it possible for two men, like Daddy and me, to get along without a woman in the house? What about the washing and the ironing and the cooking? Who scrubbed the floor? Who washed the windows? Wasn't it a shame for a growing boy like me to have to fix his own lunch to take to school because he had no mother? Every time I came into the shop, the same dumb questions.

She gave me the gladiolus, added them to our account which she kept in a journal, then reached under the counter and came up with a pie, a sweet potato pie, still warm—my favorite, and Daddy's too, which she had just happened to bake one too many of for the church supper she was getting ready to attend. She told me how long to keep it in the oven, as if she hadn't done it a thousand times before. I grabbed the pie, mumbled "thank you," and hurried out and climbed into the pickup.

Like I said before, Ike is the no-talkingest somebody in the whole world. But me? Dorasthena says I must be trying to make up the difference. But riding home in the pickup, I was too busy thinking things in my own head to open my mouth at all.

"You're not talking much, today."

"Oh, no, sir. Dr. King made this speech at the Lincoln Memorial. It's called 'I Have a Dream.' He sent me a copy, and I'm thinking about it."

"Learning another speech, is that it? Frederick Douglass, Booker T. Washington, W.E.B. DuBois—you know a lot about speeches don't you? And all of 'em by heart." He kept on driving, waiting for me to say something back, but I didn't know what to say. Dr. King was not his favorite subject. Finally he went back to being quiet. And I went back to hearing the words again, and saying them under my breath to myself.

We had turned off the highway onto an unpaved street running along between the railroad tracks on one side, and a ditch that had water in it, on the other.

"War is crazy"—all of a sudden, and from out of nowhere, Daddy spoke—"and once you been in one, it's no use trying to explain what it was like, or put it out of your mind. Korea, Korea, Korea. You can't forget it, but you just can't come right out and talk about it either. That's what I kept trying to get across to your mother, but she never understood it up to the day she died. You want to talk, but you can't, so then you want people to understand it anyway. When they don't, it makes you angry!"

Daddy had started to sweat. I don't think it was because of the heat.

"I mean, just thinking about what happened over there, about what they did to us, and what we did to them—and none of it making any sense. I get so mad that I could hit somebody, or choke somebody, any-body—a total stranger—just for the way he looked at me. Mad at the whole damn world, and especially mad at this country . . . my country. You go because they tell you to go. You fight because they tell you to fight. Then you come back, and they don't tell you anything; but you see with your own eyes that it's a lie . . . it's all a lie! Things ain't got a damn bit better for black folks. In fact, they got worse. But people still want you to grin and smile and joke about it as if you ain't been nowhere. Just sit down, make yourself comfortable, Jim Crow and all . . . putting your damn life on the line . . . and for what? For this country that talks about war like it was the weather. What the hell do they think I am?"

I had never seen him look like that or heard him talk that way before. I waited, wanting to know more about Korea, or whatever it was always nagging at the back of his mind. And maybe he would have told me, but just then a pickup truck, filled with a bunch of laughing white men standing in the back and yelling and passing a bottle around, came zooming up from behind, and pulled up alongside Daddy. It swerved and bumped into us at full speed. Daddy wrassled—wrestled—the wheel, trying to hold us on the road, but they kept on bumping us, trying to shove us over, till finally, we skidded into the ditch and slammed to a stop in water up to the hubcaps.

The truck flew on up the road, then spun all the way

round, and started back as fast as it could come. I could see their faces as they came—red, and twisted and grinning—like people drunk at a football game.

Daddy snatched open the glove compartment, grabbed out his pistol and raised it. I grabbed his hand and hung on with all my might. They were still laughing and cursing and passing the bottle around, waving a Confederate flag and yelling "Martin Luther Coon" as they came raring straight at us. Then at the last minute they swerved and were gone.

Daddy sat there a minute, flexing his fingers, looking down at his knees, sweat spilling off his face. I hadn't meant to do what I had done, stopping him that way, but I had done it. Too late to apologize now. So I didn't. Finally, he heaved a deep sigh.

"Them Edlee brothers," he said, putting the pistol back in the glove compartment. "Them and their Ku Klux friends. They jealous. They mad. Black folks been all over the television lately, getting too much attention. They ain't going to stop until they hurt somebody, you mark my word."

The motor was still running. I picked up the gladiolus from the floor where they had fallen, Daddy shifted into reverse, and inch by inch he eased us back up onto the road, and then headed on out to the cemetery.

4

Every year, on Labor Day, the Parent Teachers Association gave a school picnic out at the Elks club, way over near the golf course. It had a swimming pool, a diamond for playing softball, two tennis courts, and a miniature golf course, which nobody much used anymore. Amy Roselle always came over and prepared the hot dogs, the barbecued chicken and ribs, and a big pot of brunswick stew, and other goodies.

Most of the ladies would gather on the deck around the swimming pool, some in their bathing suits, sipping lemonade and iced tea. The men would usually be in the bar, smoking cigars and drinking beer, while us kids went down to the playroom where they had Ping-

Pong and pool tables and pinball machines for us to play with. There were plenty of records to play on the high-fi, for dancing if we wanted to. There was plenty of lemonade, fruit punch, sodas and cookies, and all kinds of good stuff all over the place.

I asked Daddy if he wanted to come when he dropped me off at the gate. But he said, "Certainly not!"

I was early, but Pearlicia was already there. I could hear her playing the piano in the ballroom upstairs. Most of the other kids hadn't showed up yet. Even Dorasthena, who had promised to meet me there, was late. Me and Billy Cabelle — Billy Cabelle and I — were playing Ping-Pong and I was beating his socks off when Pearlicia stopped playing and came downstairs and told me that Reverend Cable wanted to see me upstairs.

The bar was a big room full of bright brass trophies and pictures on the wall and shiny leather stuff. Even the walls looked like somebody had shined them with brown shoe polish. Mr. Sanford, Mollie Mae's father, who was Grand Master of the lodge, was there, sitting spread-legged, his belly hanging over his belt, smoking a cigar which he said came from South America. He had two big rings on his fingers, one of which he said was Masonic. He was the richest, most important colored man in town. The first to own a German sport car, which somebody said he paid for in cash. His hobby was cars.

Mr. Ellery, Carole's stepfather, was leaning against the bar. He was tall and thin and had worked on the railroad as a Pullman porter until he married Carole's mother, and then he didn't have to work anymore. He wore gold-rimmed glasses, and the biggest wristwatch I had ever seen. His hobby was supposed to be horses, but nobody ever saw him near one. But on holidays like this he always wore whipcord jodhpurs and tan riding boots of the most expensive leather, shined to a T. Reverend Cable; Deacon Guiness; Mr. Fenster; Mr. Maple, the undertaker; Amos Cobbs, who sold real estate; Sammy Malone and Mr. Cox, who were teachers—they were there too. I looked around for Professor Duckett, but he hadn't come yet. Usually the men would be joking and laughing, insulting each other sometimes, or talking about baseball or football or hunting and fishing. It was all in fun—but not today. Now, everybody was quiet. Looking and listening like they were children at school.

"All white people do not hate all black people. That is a lie—that is a foolishness." The grandest chair in the bar was always reserved for Mr. Mac McIllister, who got the first black student admitted to the University of Alabama. But that student's life had been in so much danger that she couldn't stay. Mr. Mac swore that one day he would bring her back. And we believed him. He was eighty years old. People laughed and said that some ol' black day he would be a judge. He certainly looked it, sitting in that chair. Usually he had the last word on everything concerning colored people, and nobody ever spoke until they were sure he was finished.

"The majority of white people are good people. Some are even our friends." He looked around the room and over his glasses, as if we all were prisoners at the bar. "People of good conscience deeply disturbed by what they see going on. But right now they are silent, timid people, ashamed of themselves, more scared of the sheriff, the Klan, and them Edlee brothers than they are of us. And now let me tell you about using our children to help us in the struggle." He shifted his cane from one hand to the other and took a sip from a tall, cold glass of lemonade while we all waited.

"I remember, in 1917, World War I, a great big race riot in East St. Louis. Crackers there objected to seeing our men in uniform. They raided the community: shooting, looting, burning right and left. A lot of black folk were killed before it was over. So the NAACP—I was in New York, a student at the Columbia Law School at the time—staged a protest march—a big, silent protest march—up Fifth Avenue, the heart of New York City. Over ten thousand people, black and white—and eight hundred of them school children—marching up Fifth Avenue in absolute silence. Nobody saying a word. All you could hear was ten thousand pairs of shoes slapping leather on that hard-hearted pavement. Marching, marching, marching. Oh, my Lord! Lots of people were skittish then too, 'cause the NAACP was using children, but we went right ahead: marching, marching, marching. That summer, when I came home, I organized the first chapter of the Alabama NAACP, right there in my office on Solomon Street, where I am to this day." He turned and looked at me. "How old are you, Stone?"

"Going on fourteen, sir."

"That's just about the average age of what we had back in 1917, fourteen years and under. I agree absolutely with Martin, we've got to involve the children in the struggle." He settled back, and took another sip, a signal that as far as he was concerned the case was closed. All the men were quiet for a moment; nobody wanted to disagree with Mr. Mac McIllister. He looked around, chuckled, and spoke again: "But excuse me, Sanford, I think you had the floor."

"I'm waiting on Cable to answer my question," Mr. Sanford said, waving his cigar and flashing the rings on his fingers. "We ain't talking about God, we talking about Martin Luther King, Jr., a man no different, no better, than you and me."

"I never said Martin was different from anybody else, and certainly Martin himself never said it."

"Naw," Mr. Ellery, who was mixing himself a drink, chimed in, "but the way you talk he might as well be. He's a good man, done more for the South, white and black, than anybody else I know. All due respects to Mr. Mac, I think this latest thing you talking about would be a big mistake—too dangerous."

"I agree," said Mr. Maple, the undertaker. "I don't mind the marching, demonstrating, picketing, and whatnot—anything to keep the pressure on these people. But when it comes to using children ain't old enough to be in high school yet, that's where I draw the line."

Mr. Fenster spoke up. His voice was thin and squeaky. "These kids ought to be in school, not out in the streets with all them crazy white people out there. I don't really think—" and then he stopped, looking around, as surprised to hear himself as everybody else.

"It's not definite," Reverend Cable said. "Martin was just wondering how you parents and teachers might feel about it as a way to dramatize the situation even more. Especially now, after the march when we got the whole world watching. I told him I'd at least talk to you all about it; but nobody planned anything definite, not as yet. How about you, Amos?"

"Well, you tell Martin for me that I for one am totally against our children out there in the line of march. Them people—they'd just as soon kill you as to look at you."

"Sam?"

"I can't understand it. What have we black folks ever done to white folks to make them hate us so?" he said, looking a little sad, and beside the point.

"Well, whatever we do, we've got to figure out a way to involve these young people. Martin insists on that." Reverend Cable kept pushing.

"Okay with me. That's okay—as long as what they get involved in ain't dangerous." Mr. Maple again.

"We know it's dangerous." Reverend Cable was trying not to sound annoyed. "Martin does, and so do I; but still, at the same time, like Mr. Mac said, we can't afford to leave them out of it altogether. Children are curious, and they're worried. They want to know what's going on, want to feel included. That's why I asked Stone, here, to talk with the young people, find out how they felt about all this, what they're thinking."

"Wait a minute, Reverend Cable," Deacon Guiness said, looking down at me. I don't think he much liked the idea of me being Junior Assistant Pastor. "Stone ain't nothing but a baby himself. They all are. They're kids. Naturally they think it's fun. They think it's excitement. What they know about danger?"

"Stone is young, but I trust him. I depend on him almost as much as I depend on you, Guiness, and you're chairman of the deacon board. What's more, the kids trust him, much more than they would you or me. Tell 'em, Stone. Tell 'em what the kids told you."

"Well," I said, "we had a sort of a little meeting: Dorasthena, PeeWee, Mollie Mae, Carole, Hookie Fenster, Pearlicia, Billy, and they said yes."

"Yes, what?" That from Mr. Sanford.

"We children don't think it's fair . . . we want to do

what Dr. King wants us to do. We want to be in the demonstrations too—even if we have to go to jail!"

Everybody started speaking at once, almost on top of one another, so fast I could hardly keep up.

"March and picket and go to jail, you say? No, sir!" That was Deacon Guiness, who hadn't marched the first time.

"No matter the dogs, the water cannons, and the billy clubs, they want to march. It's crazy!" Mr. Maple said, who hadn't been there either.

"I don't care what Mollie Mae said, she ain't going on into them streets." Mr. Sanford slammed his fist on the arm of his chair.

"And Carole ain't either."

"Pearlicia certainly is not, and neither is Billy." That was Mr. Cabelle, who runs the barbershop on Quincy Street.

"They're just kids. They have no idea what this is all about." That was Mr. Cobbs.

Reverend Cable kept on trying. "Oh yes, they do. This is about their future and they know it. And they don't want to sit on the side lines and just watch. They want to do what the Little Rock Nine did—they want to take part."

"The Little Rock Nine was high school."

"Yeah, and that was Arkansas; this is Alabama. These people are mean!"

"Mean yes, but still, they ain't no fools," Mr. Cox said, looking dead at Mr. Mac who folded his arms and looked and listened and smiled. "What with television there, looking over their shoulders, I don't think they'll touch these kids."

"So, then, you agree to let your Doris be in the march?" Mr. Cobbs jumped in again.

"No, I didn't say that, now, I didn't say that."

"And anyway, it ain't up to the kids. It's up to us. And I for one say no!" Mr. Sanford pulled out his handkerchief and blew his nose.

"Me too," said Mr. Ellery. "This thing has gotten to be too scary. The Edlee brothers, and all their Ku Klux friends, I hear they been riding around all over the county, cussing, drinking, firing off their pistols, burning crosses, talking about Martin Luther Coon."

I started to tell them about how those men had run me and Daddy off the road, but I didn't get the chance.

"Hold it. Hold it, brothers. Hold it! Let's hear from one at a time. Cable, you still have the floor," said Mr. Mac, putting himself back in the argument.

"Okay, okay. I've thought about it. I've prayed about it. And I agree. Maybe we shouldn't put children in the line of march—not right now. But suppose, first, we take them and train them. Show them what to do when they get out there. Teach them about nonviolence and how to use it to protect themselves. Set up a workshop, hold classes in creative nonviolence, explain it to them, drill them in it, step by step. How about that?"

Reverend Cable stopped, searching the faces before

him. They all seemed confused and a little embarrassed. Nobody wanted to risk being made to look foolish—certainly not in front of Mr. Mac, who bent himself forward, leaning on his cane, and also searched their faces. He looked at them, and they looked at him. And for a minute nobody said nothing—nobody said anything—not until Mr. Cox decided to take a stand.

"No, Reverend Cable, no! You tell Martin we men don't mind facing these red-neck bastards, but we'll be damned if—"

"Mind your tongue, Cox, for heaven's sake," said Reverend Cable as he looked at me.

Mr. Cox looked at me too, then snapped his mouth shut. Mr. Mac took another look at the men, then leaned back in his chair, smiling again. The verdict was coming. "Gentlemen, gentlemen—please, please. It seems as if Martin and Cable have got the court in a dither, a moral quandary. Let's take a moment and see if perhaps we can sort this thing out.

"I have before me here assembled much of the middle class colored gentry of our fair city. Ardent supporters, most of us are, of the good Reverend Martin Luther King, Jr., but only with our mouths, and sometimes our pocketbooks, but certainly not with our bodies. We all applauded—safe on the sidelines—when Dr. King led that first demonstration here in April and brought the television cameras and hence the eyes of the world to our fair city. Some of us did send money.

But few of us, distinguished gentlemen that we are, were out there in the line of march." He paused to let the indictment sink in and then went on.

"We felt the sting of the water hoses, but only from reading it secondhand in the papers. We heard the growling of the police dogs and the crunch of Bull Connor's billy clubs breaking somebody's head, but only on television. We were no closer to the struggle than people watching in London or in China. I was there, of course, but then I'm getting senile and therefore not representative or responsible for my actions. Cable was there. Fred Shuttlesworth was there. Fred Gray was there. Gomillion was there. Rosa Parks was there.

"But most of us were absent without leave. Martin, for all his passion and eloquence, couldn't move us. Oh, no, not us—even though it was our freedom, and the future of our children, that was involved. Much too busy, or otherwise engaged—that's what we were. God help us." His voice was softer now and a little sadder.

Nobody moved; nobody made a sound. They stood there, in front of Mr. Mac, like children being scolded.

"Now, when Martin calls upon our children to fall in and fill up the ranks, we suddenly rise in rebellion; we don't want them to go . . . too dangerous . . . too inconvenient. We want them to grow up safe and segregated, the same kind of Jim Crow cowards we have been for years. All Cable is suggesting is a workshop—

a classroom where our children can at least learn about struggle and how to wage it. Not by guns and bullets— you know as well as I we cannot win that way—but with civil disobedience.

"I put the question from the bench: All those in favor of slavery continued, with segregation and Jim Crow laws and being called a dirty nigger till the ending of your days, may signify by raising his hand right now. Everybody else will send his children to Cable's workshop in creative nonviolence for children. And now, Sanford, I, for one, am starving. Get me some food up here, for heaven's sake!"

Mr. Mac stood up; the session was adjourned. "Stone, go downstairs," Mr. Sanford said, glad to change the subject. "Tell the kids to get washed up. Chow will be on the table in fifteen minutes."

I ran back downstairs and found the place packed. The music was loud and everybody was dancing. Some of them were singing along at the top of their voices. I tried to speak but nobody was listening. I went to the hi-fi, turned it off, then turned to the room and held up my hand.

"Listen, everybody," I said. I was so excited about what I had to tell them I could hardly wait for them to quiet down. But before I could open my mouth, Hookie spoke up.

"PeeWee," he said, "turn that music back on."

PeeWee wasn't even near the set, so I knew what Hookie was up to.

"You heard me, PeeWee. Turn the music back on." PeeWee looked at Hookie, and then at me. And then he went and turned the hi-fi back on. But Dorasthena, just as quick, pushed PeeWee aside and turned the set back off again. Everybody stood where they were. It got completely quiet because nobody spoke. I looked at Hookie, and Hookie looked at me. PeeWee said "uh-uh," and started grinning. Then Hookie took off his coat.

"So, our little black Jesus boy here, thinks he can tell everybody else what to do."

Hookie and me—Hookie and I—were classmates, and rivals too. You see, Hookie likes Dorasthena very much, and last year he asked her to be his girlfriend. She told him to go jump in the lake. Hookie thought she did it because of me. Now when I took a vow with myself to be nonviolent just like Dr. King, PeeWee and Dorasthena were the only ones I told. But PeeWee and his big mouth . . . now everybody knew, and a lot of my friends teased me about it. But Hookie Fenster wasn't teasing, he was still mad at me.

Hookie came and stood right in my face. "PeeWee's been telling everybody," he said, "how holy Stone is. That he is going to be nonviolent no matter what for the rest of his life, just like Dr. King. Right?"

"I said I thought he was wonderful, and I wish I could be like him." My voice sounded strange and thin and my mouth got dry and my heart was beating fast.

"That ain't what you said," PeeWee spoke up. "You

said everything Martin Luther King did, you could do too."

"PeeWee," Dorasthena jumped in. "For Pete's sake, why you got to always be running your mouth?"

Everybody had stopped and was watching us, which made Hookie Fenster happy. Nothing he likes better than making fun of people, especially if they were smaller than him, like me. "So you're gonna turn the other cheek, let somebody hit you, spit in your face, maybe, and not hit back . . . for the rest of your life."

"Well, that's not exactly what I said."

"The Ku Klux Klan? . . . the Edlee brothers, Bull Connors, come up to you, hit you in your face, you could just stand there and not hit back? You could do that?"

"Well, I could try."

"Well, try it now!" And with that he pushed me so hard on the chest with the flat of his hand that if I hadn't stumbled back against the pool table, I would have fell—fallen. It was a surprise; I wasn't expecting it. It almost knocked me down.

PeeWee acted like it was the funniest thing he had ever seen. "Man, oh, man, did you-all see what Hookie just did to Stone?"

I was as mad—I mean as angry—as I have ever been in my life. But I wasn't going to let Hookie, or anybody else, cause me to lose my temper—certainly not in front of all my friends. Also I was scared. But I managed to swallow what I was feeling and turn away, deciding to ignore the both of them. And besides, as president of the Young People's Bible Class, I had a job to do.

"Reverend Cable is going to set up a workshop at Holy Oak on creative nonviolence for children . . . teach us how to defend ourselves without hurting anybody else—"

"We don't have to wait for Reverend Cable, I can teach you now!" Hookie pushed me again, this time from behind, and I fell facedown onto the pool table. He grabbed at me, but I flipped over.

"What's the matter, little black Jesus? Where's that other cheek that you're supposed to turn?" Hookie was in his glory. He started around the table. But Dorasthena snatched up a cue stick and stepped in front of him. "You hit him again, Hookie Fenster, you lay your hands on Stone just one more time, and I'll go up side your head with this cue stick, so help me God." Anybody who knows Dorasthena, knows better than to get her started. The rest of the kids moved in closer, licking their lips and waiting.

"Stay out of this, Dorasthena." I couldn't fight Hookie Fenster, not now—not with the vow I had taken, but I certainly couldn't let Dorasthena fight him for me. I took her by the arm and put her behind me, and just doing that made me feel better. I spoke like always, and didn't have to raise my voice.

"You can say anything you want, Hookie Fenster, you can do anything you want. But I'm not going to let you make me lose my temper." The room got quiet as a pin. All of a sudden, I don't know how, the kids were on my side, and Hookie knew it. He hesitated and looked around the room from side to side, and in that instant I knew I had won, not only over Hookie, but over myself. I wasn't afraid anymore, and that was the secret!

But in winning I had made Hookie look bad in front of the others. Up to now he might have been half playing, but now it was for real. Somewhere, somehow, sooner or later I knew he'd get me. Lucky for the both of us, Mr. Sanford opened the door and shouted down the stairs: "All right, you kids, come and get it."

5

School opened on Wednesday, and that was always one of the happiest days of my life. Daddy let me off at the gate. I was running almost before my feet hit the cinder path that led right up to the broad steps of the building, which was big and old and brick, with a lot of vines growing on the walls, and set way back on top of a little rise.

It used to be a high school, and behind it and a little to one side was a stadium. The games were now played at the new high school. Ike, Reverend Cable, and Professor Duckett—he's the principal here now—all had been students at Stedman when it was still a high school. That stadium was where they had played their football games. People still talked about those games sometimes. Being at Stedman was one of the ways I had of remembering my mother, who had been the head cheerleader.

And that's one of the things that made it so special to me. I looked around and felt back home again. Everybody seemed as glad as I was, scrambling around, not being able to keep still, saying hello to one another and to all the teachers. PeeWee was all over the place, showing his pictures. And though I couldn't hear him, I knew that he was making sure that everybody knew what a great bus captain he had been. Mollie Mae and Carole, each in a brand-new dress that looked expensive, were going around and handing out little presents to everybody.

Billy Cabelle was out on the playground tossing a football to Hookie Fenster, who caught the ball, turned, and threw it as hard as he could straight at me. It caught me off guard; but I snagged it anyway, and just as quick, I threw it back, nailing him dead in his chest. Then I looked at him to let him know I knew what he was up to and that I was ready, then ran to catch up with Doris Mayfield, Theresa Crump, and Morgan Heard. I didn't see Dorasthena; she would be helping Mrs. Edison. She never said, but we all knew that someday Dorasthena would be a teacher too. Students and parents and other visitors were all over, but mostly we crammed into the hallway around the water fountain. Everybody talking and nobody listening, telling each other again and again everything that had happened over the summer, especially the March on Washington.

The bell rang and everybody went to his homeroom to register. Another bell rang. Dorasthena met me in the hallway, and we all filed into the assembly hall, still talking and laughing and horsing around, throwing spitballs, playing jokes on one another, until there was a loud chord on the piano that was meant to get our attention. And it did. There was a big rush as everybody found a seat and got into it as fast as possible.

Pearlicia played while the teachers and people from the Board of Education and the PTA came in and went up onto the stage and sat in a row of chairs. Mr. Mac McIllister was already there. Then Professor Duckett, the school principal, marched in and took his place behind the lectern. He wiped his glasses, put them back on his nose, and looked out into the auditorium—just looked. And that's all he had to do—everybody got as quiet as a mouse. Professor Duckett was nice enough, always joking with us and kidding around. But we knew that when it came to being principal, he didn't take no stuff—any stuff—off anybody. He had that official professor's look he could put on his face. Everybody would know that he was not a man to be played with.

We just sat there, keeping our mouths shut, staring straight at the lectern, nobody daring to move or to say a word. Professor Duckett looked from one side of the auditorium to the other, then he nodded to Pearlicia, who struck another chord, which meant for us to stand, everybody at the same time—like soldiers. The bugle corps marched in carrying the flag. Professor Duckett led us in the pledge of allegiance, then everybody sang the Negro national anthem.

> "Lift every voice and sing,
> Till Earth and Heaven ring,
> Ring with the harmony of liberty."

The words had been written by James Weldon Johnson, and the music by his brother, J. Rosamond. It was just as important to know these names as it was to know the song. And this song was more important than any lesson in our textbooks. You had to know it letter perfect, like passing a test, and stand up straight and stick out your chest and sing just as loud as you could—or you were dead! The teachers would be busy watching our mouths, checking on who of us was singing and who was faking. They knew how to read your lips, and woe unto the one whose lips weren't moving right. That could get you punished. Your own mother might not speak to you for days, or report you to your father for shaming the family.

> "Let our rejoicing rise,
> High as the listening skies,

Let it resound,
  Loud as the rolling sea."

Professor Duckett was chubby and almost bald. His head was shiny with sweat, which he kept mopping with his handkerchief. He always wore a bright bow tie, and he usually smelled like Daddy's shaving lotion. He was always smiling a lot, going around shaking people's hands, telling jokes, and laughing louder than anybody else.

But this was serious business. He wasn't smiling now, as he introduced the members of the faculty and some city officials, some of whom had a few words to say. And some, like Mr. Mac, who had more than a few. And then he made his welcoming address, which most of us could recite from memory—all about Frederick Douglass and Harriet Tubman and Booker T. Washington and W.E.B. DuBois and Jackie Robinson and Joe Louis and Martin Luther King, Jr., and what he expected from every student here: "Excellence, excellence, and excellence again. I expect it of you. The teachers expect it of you. Your parents expect it of you. The entire Negro people expect it of you! And now, I have a few announcements to make, and then you will all rise and march out row by row and go to your home-rooms to talk to your teachers and get your assignments. Isaac Stone, Jr., please see me in my office."

Dorasthena pinched my hand. "What you up to

now?" She walked me to the office. "You better watch out for Hookie and for your good friend PeeWee too. I'll wait outside."

"For goodness sake, Dorasthena, why you always so down on PeeWee?"

"You'll find out soon enough."

Dorasthena couldn't stand PeeWee. She didn't trust him, called him a two-faced lying machine. And mostly she was right. Every time I tried to help him, he'd come up with another way to jam me up. Many times I wanted to give up, stop trying to be his friend. But Pee-Wee was like flypaper—no way in the world would he let you get rid of him. One time he followed me all the way home, begging me to give him one more chance. He even cried. But also she was just a little jealous of anybody who got too close to me.

The office was big, with lots of high windows and light brown walls. It had more trophies and banners and pictures of famous black people than it had books. One was a big blowup, hanging back of the desk, of the 1945 championship team, right after World War II, with Daddy and Josh Cable and Professor Duckett on it. And Jibby Greene and Mutts Malone. Another had a bunch of football players kidding around with Mama Lucy in her cheerleader costume, which she designed herself.

"Come in, Stone, come in, and have a seat." Professor Duckett went behind me and closed the office door, then came and sat at his desk. "I didn't see you at the March on Washington. You of all people."

"Daddy was afraid for me to go; thought something bad might happen."

"Ike Stone has changed. Oh, Lord, how he has changed." He got up from his desk, turned, and stood looking at the blowup on the wall. "You know, when I look at that picture of the championship team up there on the wall, I think about how it was back in 1945, the year we won the state championship. Me, Ike, Cable, Jibby, Mutts Malone, and Lucy McClellan, who was as big a devil as all us boys put together. By the way, you're looking more like Lucy every day."

I nodded, and he went on.

"All of us were crazy about Lucy McClellan, and she led us around by the nose, made absolute fools out of every one of us. Then married the one that nobody ever thought she'd marry, Isaac Stone. Now true, Ike was captain of the football team, and on the gridiron his record for passes caught and yardage gained has never been equaled, so naturally all the girls thought he was the cat's meow. But off the field it was a different story. I was busy watching Cable, trying to cut him out. Cable was busy doing the same thing, trying to cut me out. When all the time we should have been watching Ike—never much to say, clumsy, couldn't dance to save his life, couldn't put two words together to form a sentence. Sure Lucy flirted with him just like with all the rest of us; but she'd never marry a country clodhopper like Ike, or so we thought. That's how smart we were. How old are you, Stone?"

"Fourteen next month, Professor Duckett."

"And this is your last year here with us at Stedman. Next year you go on to high school. We'll miss you, Stone."

"And I'll miss being here at Stedman, sir."

"Now, I know you're young, Stone, but even so, it's not too soon to start thinking about what college you're going to." He reached into a drawer and brought out a file of papers. "I have your record right here: straight A student all the way. But then I'm not surprised. Lucy McClellan was straight A too, though for the life of me I never remember seeing her with a book in her hand. And Ike was no dummy. I mean, still waters run deep. That's Ike. If you know what I mean. So you come by your brains quite naturally. They would have both done very well in college. But they decided to run off, get married, and start a family. I hope that's not what you're planning to do."

"Oh, no sir."

"Now Cable tells me that you've decided to go into the ministry, become a preacher, like Martin Luther King. Is that correct?"

"Yes, sir."

"Good, good, good. We black folks wouldn't have made it without the Black Church—the most powerful institution we got. That's where most of our leaders come from. I think you've made a good choice, Stone. The ministry will be just fine for a smart young man like you."

"Thank you, sir."

"Of course, Cable is a Howard man, and Howard does have a good school of religion; but Morehouse is where Martin went. And Morehouse is where you ought to go. Don't you think so?"

"Yes, sir. I want to go to Morehouse too."

"Good boy. Good boy. And I tell you what let's do. You speak to Ike and ask him to drop in and see me, so I can get the paperwork started." He got up from his chair and came and slapped me on the back. "I intend to get you a scholarship. Even though you're not even in high school yet, it's not too early to start. I know the right people, and I say, thank God you're going to Morehouse, just like Martin." He gave me some pamphlets and a college catalog and two other books—one on Frederick Douglass and one on Booker T. Washington. "I know Negro History Week is not until February, but I've already marked out several speeches I want you to memorize."

Negro History Week was always the most important event of every school year. All students had to take part—read a poem, write an essay, play music by a black composer, or what I liked best to do: recite a famous speech by a famous person.

"If you don't mind, sir, would it be all right if I recited 'I Have a Dream' by Reverend Martin Luther King, Jr.?"

"Martin's big speech, eh? Hey, that's a wonderful idea!"

"I already know most of it by heart."

"I'll bet you do. Okay, young man, if that's what you want to do." He shook my hand then led me to the door. "By the way, Mutts and Jibby are going to visit us sometime this semester, maybe Thanksgiving, and I already told them about you. After all, you won't be the first preacher at Morehouse who played football." He shook my hand again and showed me out.

Dorasthena was waiting in the hall. "Hookie swore to PeeWee that he could make you mad enough to fight."

"Hookie's out of luck. Nobody can make me mad enough to fight." I looked up and saw the two of them coming fast in my direction. It was too late to run away, even if I wanted to. I turned to face them, trying to think of karate moves from the movies. "Here, Dorasthena, hold my books and papers." But just then, the alarm bell went off and scared the living daylights out of everybody.

We knew the fire bell would ring sometimes during fire drill, but nobody ever heard of fire drill on opening day. For a minute nothing happened; then the hallway was full, people scrambling in all directions, bumping into one another, not knowing exactly what we were supposed to do. "What's happening?" I asked Billy Cabelle. He didn't even stop, just kept on running, looking for his sister.

Then in the distance we heard sirens; fire trucks were all coming in our direction. The hall got even more crowded, people in panic, running over one another. A couple of girls fell down and one of them screamed. I grabbed Dorasthena's arm and started for the exit. A lot of the kids had the same idea, and things got really thick. We had to fight for a chance to get to the door.

Then we heard Professor Duckett's voice coming over the loudspeaker: "Boys and girls, now listen carefully: I want all of you to line up just as you do in a regular fire drill. The teachers are already on their way to lead you. So form a line as quickly as you can and march, quickly but orderly, out of the building. I've asked Pearlicia Cabelle to play us a march, so don't run—march—march out of the building, with all of the dignity and composure that people expect from Stedman Junior High."

It didn't take us long to clear the building. And then we stood and watched as the firemen and the police arrived and quickly went inside. I heard a teacher say word had just been received that someone had planted a bomb somewhere in the building and that it was set to go off right away, but I didn't know what to believe. Some of the firemen were laughing and some were joking as they went inside. They went down into the basement, and into all the classrooms, and even up on the roof. But nobody found a bomb. The firemen and the police were all white. They talked awhile among themselves about what was happening—some even smoked. But not a word was said to Professor Duckett, the teachers, or any of the rest of us—like we weren't even there—and then they left.

When Saturday came, PeeWee offered to help me with the roll call at the workshop, but I said no. I wanted Dorasthena to do it. All fifteen members of my Young People's Bible Class were there as well as kids from other places for the first meeting of the new class in creative nonviolence for children. Reverend Cable had just received a hurry-up call from Dr. King that morning, asking him to meet him in Atlanta, so he didn't have much time. But he did talk to us before he left.

"This is serious business, and it's not going to be fun and games. So, before we accept any of you into this class we've got to find out if you are suited for it—whether you can take people cursing you and spitting at you, calling you names, and even throwing things at you, turning water hoses and siccing dogs on you, or trying to beat you over the head with night sticks, and police batons. . . ."

I turned, and caught Hookie Fenster not listening to

Reverend Cable but looking straight at me. He balled up his fist and held it under his chin for me to see. It was plain that sooner or later I would have to fight him. I wasn't scared of him anymore but Hookie was big, and he could be dangerous. I had to force myself to listen to Reverend Cable.

"Do you have it in you to be strong enough," he continued, "disciplined enough to let people strike you and not strike back? As I said, nonviolence is not easy, but it's not too early to learn."

"I can learn it, Reverend Cable. I can do everything you said." That was PeeWee. Reverend Cable ignored him and kept right on.

"So, for the next few weeks, every Saturday, we're going to have these classes. Some of you will pretend to be marchers. Others will pretend that you are Bull Connors and his police. We'll show you how to march and keep on marching, how to protect yourself from injury, how to fall if you have to without hurting yourself."

Reverend Cable was talking slower than he usually does, and as he talked he looked each one straight in the eyes.

"Those of you who can stick it out—who can prove to my satisfaction that you have got the stuff—will be given a certificate, signed by Dr. King himself, and you will be among those selected to participate in the marches and demonstrations that Dr. King is planning.

Those of you who cannot manage it will have to be excused. Is that clear?"

He waited for an answer, but nobody spoke.

"I want you to put your names on the list that Stone is going to pass among you. And look, it's no disgrace to change your mind. That's all right too. You can leave the class now or at any time, if it gets to be too much for you. Nobody will be angry or disappointed or call you a coward. And if he does, he will have to deal with me. I say it again. Anybody who thinks that maybe this is more than you want to bite off, raise your hand."

And nobody raised a hand.

"Fine, just fine. After you sign, Stone will also give you a form we want you to take home to your mother and father. They will have to sign too. Now, if there are any questions, anything that you don't understand, tell it to Stone, and he will pass it on to me. I've got to run to Atlanta, but I'll be back in time for Sunday School tomorrow morning, and I want to introduce you all as the Creative Nonviolence Workshop for Children— the first of its kind—to the whole congregation, so they can be as proud of you young people as Martin and I are. I want to see every one of you there, and on time."

Everybody applauded, and then he left.

I finished giving out the forms then took the list with everybody's name on it downstairs to Reverend Cable's office. And then I went to the toilet, but when I pushed the door to go out I couldn't open it. I tried the door again. I rattled the doorknob, but it still wouldn't budge. Then I heard giggling out in the hall and voices whispering. But I recognized them anyway: PeeWee and Hookie and Roscoe. They had stuck a chair, or something, against the door, up under the doorknob.

"I know you're out there, PeeWee, and you too, Hookie, so you better open this door."

Nobody answered. I beat against the door with my fist as hard as I could, but the toilet was in a faraway place next to the furnace. Nobody could hear me unless they were down in the basement too. I called out again, but all I heard was whispers and giggling. Finally I got mad—I mean angry! I beat on the door with my hands until they began to hurt, and then I bumped my hip against it, again and again, until finally whoever it was moved whatever was holding it, and when I hit the door this time it flew open and I came sprawling out. I butted into somebody and down we went to the floor, me on top. It was PeeWee, of course, although I could barely make him out. He kicked and scratched like a demon. Once I did manage to pull myself free and was almost to my feet when somebody—I'm sure it was Hookie—grabbed my shoulders from behind and pushed me back down.

I tried to get hold of PeeWee's flying fists, but when I grabbed one he hit me in the eye with the other. I felt the blood gush from my nose and couldn't see a thing, and then I really tried to hurt him. I grabbed him by the throat and banged his head against the floor, like I had seen on television. I'm glad Deacon Guiness came down and switched on the light and saw us. I'm glad he managed to pull me up off PeeWee, else I might have done something I would be sorry for for the rest of my life! But mostly I felt shame; Hookie and PeeWee had finally made me break my vow.

Sunday morning Dorasthena met me at the side door to the basement as usual. Deacon Guiness was with her, waiting too. He had that look on his face and said Reverend Cable wanted to see me in his office right away. Dorasthena wanted to come with me, but Deacon Guiness told her it was private.

I could see that Reverend Cable was angry. He waited patiently as Deacon Guiness looked at me and told him the story again. "I always thought that Stone, here, could be trusted—depended on; thought he had more sense than be fist fighting here in the house of the Lord . . . thought he was different from the others, more of an example, like you thought he was. But, like they say, maybe children should be seen and not heard."

"That will be all, Deacon Guiness."

After Deacon Guiness left, Reverend Cable just sat there trying to control his temper. I started to speak, but he wouldn't let me.

"You, Stone, my Junior Assistant Pastor, a fist fight down here in the basement. Is that what you mean by nonviolence?"

"No, sir, but . . . Well, sir, some of the fellows, they decided to play a sort of prank on me, and—"

"I've already dealt with PeeWee. Told him to get out of my sight and stay out of my sight until I send for him. And I haven't the slightest idea when that's going to be. And now, here you come, looking even worse. Unless you can come up with a better excuse than Pee-Wee did, I am going to suspend you, too. Do you hear me, Stone?"

"Yes, sir, but like I was trying to say, sir—"

"PeeWee I can understand. PeeWee is a fool, but you, Stone, you, of all people, you! What kind of leader do you think you are? What kind of an example for the other kids to follow? You, down on the floor fighting like dogs, right here in my church!"

Suddenly a blast shook the building. It knocked Reverend Cable out of his chair and threw me against the bookcase. "A bomb . . . a bomb! My God, it must be a bomb!"

Reverend Cable was down on the floor, and I went to help him up. There was a funny smell and the lights blinked. We tried to get out of the office, but the door was jammed. Reverend Cable kicked it several times before it would open.

Out in the hallway we could hardly see. The screaming was coming from the right, and that's the way we ran. But there was no way I could keep up with Reverend Cable and his long legs.

The screams kept getting louder, and in a minute the hallway was full, people bumping into one another, scrambling in all directions, not knowing what to do but trying to do it anyway.

"What's the matter . . . what happened?" I asked as I stumbled up against somebody who answered as he pushed on down the hallway.

"Somebody bombed the Young People's Bible Class!" I tripped and fell to the floor and hit something sharp, which tore a hole in the knee part of my Sunday suit. I got to my feet, then looked around expecting somehow to see Dorasthena who would tell me what was happening as she usually does, but she was nowhere to be seen.

Big Mother, with flour dough all over her arms, came running out of the kitchen. "Oh, my God, it's the children," she said. She ran up the hall with me right behind her. It was loud and noisy, with people everywhere, asking one another what had happened, trying to find out where the screams were coming from. I wondered most of all where Dorasthena was—knowing all the time that she had to be in the classroom with the rest of the Young People's Bible Class, but calling her name anyway.

Our classroom—where everybody was finally heading—was at the end of the hallway against the outside basement wall. That's where the bomb had been planted. It had to be a bomb from the great big muffled sound that it had made. What else could it be? But getting to it was like trying to swim when the water's going the other way, with everybody running, pushing, and shoving things and other folks aside. Two people tripped and fell down right in front of me. One of them screamed. Lucky it was in the daytime—we could still see, but not very well. The smoke and the dust were getting thicker. The dust was making me cough as we fought our way over some chairs and a bookshelf that had fallen to the floor blocking our way. The screams were sounding more urgent and helpless; and I hoped whoever it was it wouldn't be Dorasthena. I kept on calling her name, but a lot of other people were also calling somebody. So in all the noise I could hardly hear what I was saying.

Our classroom had started off as a small chapel partitioned off from the rest of the basement by painted cinder blocks. It had a door, which somebody had already pulled off the hinges. Everybody was trying to get through to the inside where the bomb had gone off. And where people were already digging and clawing and pulling, trying to reach through a pile of broken benches and rubble and plaster from the ceiling to where the screams were coming from. I pushed my way inside and saw Reverend Cable and some of the other grown-ups digging at the bricks with bare hands. I didn't see Dorasthena, but there was Hookie Fenster lying in a corner with Mr. Fenster bending over begging him to wake up. Deacon Grantham, our Sunday School teacher, was lying on the floor covered with blood—a bench had fallen across his shoulder. Roscoe and I, we managed to pull him out and also Pearlicia from under a table.

"Have you see Dorasthena?"

Roscoe was crying, and he put his hand to an open wound on the back of his head which was bleeding. The place was so crowded you couldn't tell at first who was hurt and who was trying to help. Some of the parents had got there before me, and they were calling the names of their children.

I pushed my way through to the front of the room, and there in a corner, hiding under a desk, was Dorasthena. She looked dazed. When I called her name, she didn't answer. I moved the desk and helped her to her feet. I pulled at her arm, but she snatched it away and pointed. In the opposite corner we saw Reverend Cable and Deacon Guiness pull Mollie Mae and Carole from under the wood and brick and stuff and carry them upstairs. But it was too late. You could tell from the way their arms were dangling that they were dead. And Mrs. Sanford screamed and screamed and screamed! And then I remembered Daddy's awful dream.

6

The main thing was trying to keep from crying. When Mama Lucy died, and we were at the funeral, Daddy just sat there, quiet and stiff in the pew with me. I kept watching him to figure out what I was supposed to do, but he never moved. Never even looked in my direction, just straight ahead. Some of Mama's family had come over from Louisiana and Georgia and some of Daddy's people from Mississippi, but I didn't talk to them. I hardly knew who they were. So I felt it was just Daddy and me sitting there. He didn't cry, and I tried not to, but finally I did. And I promised myself that, no matter what, that would not happen again. Not if I could help it. If Daddy could show how much of a man he was by not crying, then so could I.

Besides, I was a pallbearer for Mollie Mae, and I had

never heard of a pallbearer breaking all down and crying like the other people. Pallbearers had a certain responsibility to hold themselves together—just like an usher. But it was hard.

I stole a glance at Dr. King, who was sitting in the pulpit. Dorasthena, me, PeeWee, Roscoe, and most of the rest of the class were sitting together in the church. But Hookie was in the hospital. He had lost an eye, and his right leg had to be taken off above the knee; but the doctor said he would live. Pearlicia and Billy had to take sleeping pills, so their parents wouldn't let them come.

Dorasthena had been there sitting right in the front row when it happened, with no idea how she wound up under the upturned desk in the corner, but she wasn't hurt, not even a scratch. She couldn't get over it, she said. It made her feel like a cheat or a traitor. She cried so hard that one of the nurses had to come and take her outside.

Carole's hair had been scorched on one side, and her face had a bandage on it, but Mollie Mae looked like she just fell asleep in a flower bed. The whole church was covered with flowers, almost hiding the two white caskets which stood in front of the pulpit side by side. Both Carole and Mollie Mae were dressed in pink, and both had on long white lace gloves. Mollie Mae had a little Bible in her hand with her named spelled in gold letters. Carole held a rosary of large, beautiful beads.

The church was packed, filled to overflowing, and

for the first time I saw some white people standing in the back. Some of them cried too. Television cameras were lined up against the wall, with newspaper people popping their flashbulbs in everyone's face. Dr. King gave the eulogy, but to tell the truth I don't remember a word he said. It was getting harder and harder for me not to cry.

The choir sang a hymn, and everybody stood up. Reverend Cable gave the prayer, but it got so hard for him to talk that he couldn't finish it. He turned and went and sat down and buried his face in his big black hands. The congregation sat down, too, and for a moment, nobody did anything or said anything, until Big Mother started in to sing "We Shall Overcome" with a voice so soft at first that nobody could hardly hear her. Then little by little other people began to join in, then the organ, playing real soft, and the piano, until before long everyone in the church was singing. Dr. King stood up, and Reverend Cable stood up. Then the two of them joined hands. People all over the church got up, too, joined hands and sang and sang and sang. Somebody took my hand. I think it was Pee-Wee, who was also a pallbearer, but my eyes were too full to see, and I was almost choking. So I snatched my hand away and went running up the aisle as fast as I could.

Outside, the sidewalk was jammed with people listening to the song on the loudspeakers that had been set up. They had joined hands and were singing "We

Shall Overcome." Across from the church was a long line of policemen, some on horses, some in riot helmets and carrying billy clubs.

I kept running till I found Daddy's pickup. He opened the door and held out his hands. I climbed in, and Daddy took me in his arms, and I laid my head on his chest, and then, I just couldn't help it: I cried like a baby.

It was four days after the funeral, and it looked to me like time hadn't even bothered to move. Everything moping around from day to day. And though each morning he'd get up before daybreak and go out and make the rounds, looking for work, it wasn't long before I'd hear Daddy and his pickup pulling back into the yard. Almost as if he was afraid to leave me home alone. And the first thing out of his mouth when he looked at me was "Them Edlee brothers!" He'd bet his life that they were the ones behind it.

Four long days—on a Monday, it was, and I had cooked breakfast but neither of us ate. After a while I asked Daddy if, maybe, I could go back to Holy Oak today.

"What for? What's happening at Holy Oak?"

"Nothing, that I know of."

"And what about school?"

"No school today. I could take the bus."

"No. No, I'm not doing anything; besides it's . . . it's

. . . I'm not sure I want you out there by yourself. I got a strong feeling this thing ain't over yet. Come on, I'll drive you there."

A lot of other people had already got there before us. For days they had been coming, standing around in little bunches, talking, looking from time to time toward the church, at the place where it happened. The police, the sheriff, newspaper and television people, people I had never seen before—coming and going into and out of the building.

And that bothered me. I wanted to be here in the worst sort of way. I needed to be here. It was my church, something I felt private and protective about. Like it was a personal friend or a part of the family. But they got there ahead of me, these strangers, and made me feel left out, and I didn't like it.

You couldn't see from the outside where the bomb had gone off. That was downstairs, below the ground, but people looked anyway. Through the windshield I saw Roscoe Malone and Billy Cabelle, sort of wandering around, looking a little lost, like everybody else. But they didn't see me. And I didn't want to see them. Not yet.

"Go ahead, if you want to. I'll wait," Daddy said.

The pickup was parked at the curb across the street and down the block a little. But I didn't feel like getting out. For the longest time, Daddy and I just sat there looking, thinking about it, but not talking.

Dorasthena came to the side of the pickup. "What's happening over at the church?" I think she too felt like something had come between her and something she loved, and she wanted to grieve about it. But how could you do that in front of all these strangers?

"I don't know. People just looking, I reckon," I said.

"Yeah. Some of them people I never even seen before."

"I suppose Reverend Cable is there, down in his office?"

"Maybe he is. I haven't seen him. I saw Pearlicia. She's inside somewhere. You going in?"

"I don't think so. I was, but now I don't think I want to."

"I don't think I want to either. I been here almost an hour, but now I think I'm going back home."

"Me too."

"Hop in, Dorasthena," Daddy leaned over me and opened the door. "We'll drop you off."

I moved to the middle, and Dorasthena climbed in and Daddy drove off. Nobody said anything, until finally Dorasthena spoke. "We ought to do something, Stone, us children, especially us in the Young People's Bible Class. Mollie Mae, Carole, and Hookie—they were our classmates; we got to do something." Dorasthena's eyes were red, so I knew she had been crying. She sounded as if she was trying not to start again.

"Do what?"

"How am I supposed to know?" There she was, using her voice to make somebody feel guilty. "Us children; something on our own. Let them people know we ain't scared, in spite of what they did. We got to do something; something big!"

I didn't feel like arguing, but after we dropped her off and started back across the train tracks, I thought about it too. Dorasthena was right. Crying wasn't enough. Us children—we children—never mind the grown-ups—we ought to do something of our own. The more I thought about it, the more I agreed. We ought to do something big . . . something important. But I hadn't the slightest idea as to what that something might be.

When Dorasthena gets something on her mind she wants somebody to do, there's no stopping her. Especially if it's me. She even called me at home and started in again, as if I was keeping her waiting. "I'm thinking about it, Dorasthena." And I was. But my mind felt funny and wasn't working so good.

For the rest of the week I felt that way, only worse. Nothing that was happening to me seemed to be happening for any reason or to make any sense at all. School was like it was closed. Most of us went, but nobody mentioned the lesson or opened any books, not even the teachers. A lot of people stayed home from work and just went around, walking the streets, maybe talking about one thing, but really thinking another—about what happened that Sunday morning. Somebody had sneaked into the basement, pretending to be a delivery man or something, and planted a bomb where the Young People's Bible Class was meeting. One whole side of the inside basement wall had been blown away. Mollie Mae and Carole had been killed, and Hookie Fenster wounded bad enough so that he had to go to the hospital. Somebody who thought that that kind of thing would scare black people and stop us from trying to get our rights like everybody else.

Reporters from the television and the newspapers were still in town. You could see them all over the place trying to talk to people: to Reverend Cable, and to Mollie Mae's father and mother, and also Carole's parents, and to anybody else they could find. But nobody much wanted to talk, so most folks didn't. Just stood around in bunches, looking and wondering and waiting. There was one picture on television that everybody did talk about: one of the Edlee brothers. The police had picked him up on suspicion and questioned him about the bombing. But then they turned him loose. And there he was with a mouthful of chewing tobacco, drooling and grinning, and spitting all over the television.

I kept going over everything in my mind. I couldn't stop. I couldn't sleep, but lay there on the bed with tears in my eyes, trying as hard as I could to disbelieve, to make the whole thing go away, and not be true. I was right there when it happened—one of the first to get there, and dig through the mess and the smoke and the noise and help pull people out. I saw it all with my eyes. Still, I kept trying to keep it from being real. It was impossible to really believe that there was a bomb planted in the church basement classroom. And might have killed me, if I had been where I should have been. The more I thought of it, the more everything got strange. I never felt this loose and dizzy in my life, not even when Mama Lucy died. I suppose that's why I can't for the life of me remember who first came up with the idea of having a march for Mollie and Carole and Hookie. A children's march, all our own.

It started small, but little by little, the whole thing began to take shape, until, finally, all at once, all us kids were talking about it and nothing else. Almost as if everybody had come up with the same idea at the same time. The children's march became our secret thing. And the more we talked about it, the more we knew—no matter what the grown-ups said—it just had to happen. Reverend Cable was out of town, and anyway, maybe the first person we thought we ought to try it out on was Hookie Fenster.

I couldn't look at PeeWee without feeling sorry for what I had done. His face was still puffy under the eye, and I certainly wasn't angry at him anymore. The three of us—PeeWee and Dorasthena and I, we sort of appointed ourselves the organizing committee and headed straight for the hospital. Dorasthena got as far as the door, but refused to go any farther.

"Don't stay too long. Remember we still got to get out to the cemetery before dark."

"Aw, come on, Dorasthena, I thought Hookie Fenster used to be your boyfriend," Pee Wee said.

"Shut up, PeeWee, and anyway I got to call Miss Rhettis to see if Reverend Cable is back yet. I'll wait on the bench by the bus stop."

"I don't get it," PeeWee said. "She ain't afraid to go to the cemetery. As a matter of fact, it's her idea. So how come she won't come inside the hospital?"

"Her grandmother died in this hospital. Had cancer."

"Well, at least she was better off than me. I never even knew who my mother was," said PeeWee, trying to look sad.

We went to the desk, got the visitors cards, and went up to the ward and into Hookie's room. He had so many bandages you could hardly tell it was him—it was he. You could see his nose and left cheek and one eye. And that was shut. Like he was asleep. Mr. Fenster was there sitting in a corner, looking at the pictures in *Ebony* magazine. His suit, which was always too big, swallowed him up even more. He looked smaller and frailer than I had ever seen him look. He seemed glad to see us, as if he needed company more than Hookie. Daddy said you could look right at Mr. Fenster and never even notice he was there.

"Hookie's asleep; going in and out ever since I been here, talking out of his head. But that's because they got him doped up pretty heavy. I hope you fellows can stay with him a little while, long enough for me to go outside and have a smoke."

His tiny hands had a whole lot of veins on the back, and they trembled as he opened the door and went out. "I won't be long."

I sat down in the chair he left and picked up the magazine. PeeWee went and stood by the bed staring down at Hookie's face. Suddenly he shouted: "Hey, Stone, come look. His eye is moving. I think he's waking up."

I got up to look, and sure enough Hookie opened his eye and rolled his head from side to side and tried to talk. But it wasn't exactly words coming out of his mouth, just sounds that didn't make sense. He moved his right arm out from under the cover, and it was bandaged too, all the way down, except for the fingers.

PeeWee shouted even louder. "Hey Hookie . . . Hookie, it's me . . . PeeWee Higginbottom. Me and Stone. We come to see you. Find out how you doing. And tell you the news."

Hookie closed his eye, and he kept moving his head from side to side. He raised his hand, and I reached out and took it. He squeezed my hand, and then he opened his eye and looked at me as if he knew me.

"Guess what, Hookie! Guess what me and Stone and all the rest of us are going to do. . . . Have a march, a children's march—just classmates and stuff—maybe no grown-ups at all. How about that?"

But I don't think Hookie was listening. He closed his eye again as he turned his head to one side. His hand went limp and slipped out of mine. And he was asleep again.

Dorasthena had called the church and found out that Reverend Cable was there. So after we left the hospital we went to Holy Oak, where a lot of things were still happening but not nearly as much as before. First thing, when we got downstairs, we went by the classroom, hoping to go inside and see where the bomb had exploded, but it was still roped off. The people from the insurance company told us we could stand and look, but not to go too close and not to touch anything.

It was an awful mess of plaster, glass, wooden splinters, and a big hole blown in the outside wall, part of which had collapsed. You could see the beams where some of the ceiling had fallen, and the electric wires and water pipes. One of Carole's white shoes was still there under a pile of papers, all of it under a bench that had fallen over on its back. Somebody's pocketbook, open and empty, was hanging on the back of a caved-in chair. Paper was everywhere: from Sunday School books mostly, but also from hymnals and Bibles and pictures of holy places and Martin Luther King, Jr., and posters of people from the Bible on the wall. Spots of dried blood were on the floor, and a quarter, a dime, and two pennies were under a table, just beneath the rope. PeeWee knelt down, reached in, and picked them up when the insurance people weren't looking. But Dorasthena smacked his hand and made him put them back.

"Come on," I said. "Let's talk to Reverend Cable." We headed down the hall.

"What if he says no?" Dorasthena asked.

"Yeah, Stone . . . What would we do then?" said PeeWee.

"Reverend Cable is our friend, but he's so busy that sometimes he doesn't always understand." I tried to sound as if it would be easy, but I was thinking too. Grown-ups are very set in their ways, and they don't like to listen to us much, except—like PeeWee said—to make sure we know what it is they want us to do. It was supposed to be our march, a children's march, something all our own. We had to make sure everybody understood that—without hurting their feelings, especially Reverend Cable.

"Maybe we ought to go into the rec room first, and talk, plan things out, get our story together. Then we can tell Reverend Cable exactly what we want and not waste his time." That's what Dorasthena suggested and that's what we did. She went into the rec room and we followed her.

We came up with ideas to spare, and every one was bigger and better than the rest. It didn't take us long to work the whole thing out.

School children from all over the city would march from their schools to Stedman Stadium, where we would have a program in honor of Carole and Mollie Mae and Hookie Fenster. Grown-ups could take part if they wanted to; but it was our march. That was the main thing. There would be music, but that we could leave to Pearlicia. Thelma Dodd would sing "Precious Lord, Take My Hand." PeeWee would be Grand Marshall. He would see that every classroom and teacher in the march knew where to stand once they got to the stadium. Dr. King would be asked to come and lead the march. Reverend Cable would say the invocation, Professor Duckett would say a few words on behalf of the school, and I would recite Dr. King's I Have a Dream speech.

The more we talked and planned, the more excited we got. "Hurry up," I said, finally. "We've got to talk to Reverend Cable before he leaves for somewhere else again." We went back through the hall, past the kitchen where Big Mother was busy polishing the stove. The door to the office was open, so we went right on in.

Reverend Cable was sitting in his chair behind the desk. He had a thermometer stuck in his mouth. He started to say something when he saw us coming, but

Doc Wheeler, a big, tall, brown-skinned man, was taking his blood pressure and telling him to shut up.

"Cable, I'll bet you ain't been taking them pills like I told you. You don't slow down and take it easy you gonna have a heart attack, or a stroke—or both."

Reverend Cable snatched the thermometer out of his mouth. "Whoever said you were a doctor?"

Doc Wheeler grabbed the thermometer and shoved it back into Reverend Cable's mouth. "Shut up, Cable, or the next voice you hear will be your local undertaker. Your temperature is okay, but everything else is awful. When are you going to do like I tell you, and quit trying to save the Negro race all by yourself?"

He stopped to light the stump of a cigar he always had in his mouth, then folded up his blood pressure machine and put it back into his bag. His cigar stank. Every time he came to Stedman to give us shots or something, Professor Duckett made him leave it outside.

He took a pad from his pocket and began to write on it. "I can't keep making this prescription stronger, you know. And even if I did it won't do any good if you don't slow down, eat right, and take better care of yourself." He ripped the paper off the pad and handed it to Reverend Cable, then snapped his bag shut. "And by the way"—taking the soggy cigar out of his mouth —"this is one I heard in Dothan about glass-eyed Susie with the wooden leg. You children better shut your ears."

But before he could say any more, a stout white lady with gray hair and beads around her neck, a walking cane, and glasses with a ribbon hanging down marched into the office. She was followed by a thin, tall, stooped-over white man who looked like he didn't have much blood, and no hair at all.

"I am Mrs. Tucker Stribling, and this is Purdy, my secretary. We've come to see the bombing. And who are you?"

"I am Reverend Joshua Cable, I'm pastor here at Holy Oak. And this is Doctor Robert E. Lee Wheeler."

"How do you do."

"How do you do."

"And here are three members of our Young People's Bible Class: Dorasthena Foster, Isaac Stone, and Peter Paul Higginbottom."

"How do you do." The three of us spoke up together.

"We came to see this awful thing that has happened. It makes me sick to my stomach—and also to bring you this. Purdy." She turned to the thin, no-colored man who stood beside her. He handed Reverend Cable a fat little pouch with drawstrings on it.

"Here is the sum of two hundred seventy-one dollars and thirteen cents." Reverend Cable looked at the bag, but didn't know what to say.

"You can count it, if you want to. . . . It's all there."

"Thank you . . . thank you very much. Oh, no, no need for that."

Doc Wheeler looked for a place to put out his cigar stump, but couldn't find one, so he put it back into his mouth, then stood watching.

"That was the collection taken up at Mrs. Tucker Stribling's insistence at the Wayside Presbyterian Church on Market Street, last Sunday after we heard the news. And this"—Mr. Purdy reached into his inside coat pocket—"is a personal check from Mrs. Stribling herself in the sum of two hundred twenty-eight dollars and eighty-seven cents, bringing it up to a grand total of five hundred dollars, to help in the repair of your church."

"We at Wayside think what happened to those children Sunday before last—the Lord's day—was despicable! And we want you to know that there are some good, decent white people in this city who simply do not hold with such goings-on against the colored. Now may we see where it happened?"

"Thank you, Mrs. Stribling," Reverend Cable said, putting the money and the check in the drawer of his desk. "And, thank you, Mr. Purdy, and thanks, also, to the entire membership at Wayside Presbyterian. My congregation will be very pleased, I'm sure, to receive this great offering in the generous, Christian spirit in which it was given. But the insurance examiners, and some men from the FBI, are looking things over, trying to assess the damages, and they are asking us all to stay out of the way until they're finished."

"How did it happen?" Mrs. Stribling was still curious.

"There's always people coming in and out of this basement. It was easy enough for somebody to sneak in and plant the bomb, then be on his way."

"I've got to be going, Cable." Doc Wheeler picked up his bag. "Very nice to have met you, Mrs. Stribling. Mr. Purdy. And don't forget, Josh, you better do like I tell you and get yourself some rest, or the next voice you hear may be from your God." He laughed, put on his hat, then took it off again and started out. He bumped into a white man who had his hat on, who had to step aside to let him pass.

"Which one of you is Reverend Cable?" the man asked.

"I am."

"I'm from Southern Amalgamated Insurance. We need you for a minute or two—won't take but a second. Would you mind?"

"Of course not. Stone, you and Dorasthena and Pee-Wee make Mrs. Stribling and Mr. Purdy comfortable. Get them a soda—or ask Big Mother if she can spare some coffee. I'll be right back." He left with the insurance man.

Dorasthena offered to get our guests whatever they wanted from the kitchen. They didn't want anything. We stood around for a moment trying to think up something that grown-ups would say, but we couldn't.

"Did you all know the two little colored girls who got killed?" Mrs. Stribling asked.

It was sort of a silly question. This was probably the first time she had ever been inside a colored church. So I could understand if she was nervous.

"Oh, yes, ma'm," I said. "We were all in the Young People's Bible Class together."

"And also they were our classmates at Stedman Junior High," Dorasthena added.

PeeWee opened his mouth, but I stepped on his toes before he could say anything. I wanted us to keep quiet and wait for Reverend Cable, but Mrs. Stribling kept talking.

"Well, I can't tell you how undone I was . . . how absolutely shocked that something this awful should happen in our city." She started toward the chair. Mr. Purdy moved to help her, but she pushed him away. "Purdy, here, his family was Confederate—fought for slavery. His great-grandfather was an adjutant on the staff of General Robert E. Lee. Right, Purdy?"

"Yes, Mrs. Tucker Stribling. But that don't mean we Purdys have any truck with low-life trash that would do such an evil thing. How ever must we look to the rest of the civilized world?" Mr. Purdy looked sad and wiped his face with his handkerchief.

"But we Tuckers, my folks, we fought for the Union, against the slaveholders. Did you know that there were more than a thousand white boys from Alabama who went and joined the Union Army? They didn't believe in slavery, or anything having to do with slavery, and neither do I. It just makes me so mad I could spit! Some red-neck lowlife, putting a bomb in a church house just because the people are a different color. . . . Now you tell me, Purdy, you tell me—what on earth is the Southland coming to?"

"God only knows, Mrs. Stribling, 'cause I sure don't."

Then PeeWee had to open his big mouth. "We planning a march—biggest march this city has ever seen. School children—from all over the city."

"Oh, hush up, PeeWee, nobody asked you nothing," Dorasthena said, looking hot bullets.

"A march? . . . What kind of march?" Mrs. Stribling asked.

"A children's march, in memory of our friends, from all the schools all over town, and stuff. Just by ourselves, no grown-ups allowed."

"Ooooo, PeeWee, that's not so, and you know it," Dorasthena said. "Why you want to tell that big ol' lie? Grown-ups can too come if they want to."

I signaled them both behind Mrs. Stribling's back to shut their mouths. We hadn't even asked Reverend Cable. But it was too late. Mrs. Stribling was getting all excited.

"A children's march . . . a children's march indeed. Well now, Purdy, and what do you think of that?"

Mr. Purdy had to swallow twice. "Well, thank God I am a Christian, and I don't personally hold with violence—certainly not with planting a bomb in a colored house of the Lord. But there are some awful people out there who don't feel like you and me, Mrs. Stribling. Feelings on this racial thing are running mighty high. People think that maybe none of this would have happened if people from the outside hadn't come into our community and started to stir things up."

"You mean Martin Luther King?"

"Well, Mrs. Tucker Stribling, even you have to admit that nothing like this ever happened before he came to our city."

"Nonsense. It was bound to happen, Martin King or no. Jim Crow is dead. There's nothing you can do, Mr. Purdy—or I, for that matter—to bring it back, and I thank God for that. Good riddance, I say, and it's about time! These children want to march, I say let them march; that's what I say."

Just then, Reverend Cable hurried back into the room.

"I was just telling these children," Mrs. Stribling continued, "that over one thousand Alabamians, including my grandfather, L. Benjamin Tucker, fought on the Union side in the War Between the States. And when it was over and they came back, they ran into the same kind of riff-raff low-life behavior, just like you and your people have. Even the quality folks refused to speak to them. Did you know that? One time ol' Ben, him and a few of his men, marched down the streets as big as you please on the Fourth of July, wearing their Union Army uniforms. I was just a little girl at the time, but I remember people jeering at them, spitting at them, throwing rotten eggs and calling them damn Yankees and nigger lovers! Oh, you colored aren't the only ones that got the back of the hand from people in this town. And I say exactly what my grandpa would have said: If these children want to march through the streets in honor of the memory of their murdered friends, I say let them march."

"March?" Reverend Cable was completely puzzled. "I'm not quite sure I—"

"They've just been telling us about the children's march, and I think it's wonderful!"

Reverend Cable was looking straight at us—and I didn't like what I saw in his eyes. "Well, this is the first time I'm hearing anything about it."

"And if anybody tries to stop them—the sheriff, the police, or any of that low-life riff-raff trash, tell them to come and see me, Mrs. Tucker Stribling. And now, Reverend, Purdy and I would like to see the bombing."

"Yes, Mrs. Stribling, yes, of course. But you—Stone, Dorasthena, PeeWee—you three stay right here. Don't you move till I get back."

He left with Mrs. Stribling and Mr. Purdy. Dorasthena jumped down PeeWee's throat. "You see there, you little fool, you little idiot? See what you have done? Who told you to open your mouth!" PeeWee ducked, although she hadn't even raised her hand.

He opened his mouth, trying to defend himself, but with Dorasthena that was impossible. He couldn't get a word in. When Reverend Cable got back he was so mad he was changing colors. Lucky for us, just at that minute, the phone rang and he picked up the receiver.

"Yes, this is Cable. . . . Dr. King? Yes. Put him on." He calmed down at once. While his back was turned, the three of us almost fell over each other scrambling to get out of Reverend Cable's office as fast as we could. We didn't slow down until we got to Mrs. Ellis's flower shop.

Dorasthena is always busy doing things that nobody else would think of. For instance, at the funeral the church was full of flowers from grown-ups, but not a single flower from any of us children. She didn't think that was right; she didn't think that was fair. And, being Dorasthena, she set off to do something about it. First, she went to Mrs. Ellis and ordered something special—a big floral wreath that we could carry out to the cemetery and put on the graves of our classmates. Then she went around to all us students and class-mates, and even some of the teachers, and collected money. She didn't raise as much as she needed; but nobody—certainly not Mrs. Ellis—can say no to Dor-asthena. The way she can beg and whine and make other people feel guilty!

"All right. I'll let you young folks owe me this time, but if I don't get my money by the first of the month, I am going straight to your parents."

The wreath was big and green and red, with white and pink and purple colored flowers. It had a big satin sash across the middle with Mollie Mae's and Carole's names, and said Rest in Peace, from all your classmates at Stedman Junior High. It was so big it almost took the three of us to carry it to the bus stop.

Dorasthena was so mad at PeeWee—I mean, angry at him—that she told him to go home and quit following us and never let us see his face again, else she was liable to go upside his head with her fist so hard it would knock his brains out through his other ear. Pee-Wee begged and promised never to open his mouth again.

"Never mind your promises," Dorasthena said. "Everybody knows what a big liar you are." I tried to help him out, but she got mad at me too. Finally, I had to tell her if PeeWee didn't go, I wouldn't go either, and she'd have to take the wreath to the cemetery all by herself.

PeeWee grinned from ear to ear, looking as if he had won a big victory. "Go sit on the bench, PeeWee, and hold the wreath," I said. "I want to talk to Dorasthena." He went and sat down.

"You think PeeWee is your best friend, don't you? Well he ain't." Dorasthena pouted.

Of course PeeWee's not my best friend. Dorasthena is, and she knows it. It's just that her feelings were hurt.

"Look, Dorasthena," I said, trying to explain. "Pee-Wee's a runt. He wants more than anything in this world that people respect him, and nobody does.

Nobody pays any attention to him, or if they do, it's only to laugh at him. How do you think you'd feel if somebody was always putting you down like that? PeeWee's just trying to prove that he can be a man, and he's got nobody to show him how."

"Nobody but you, huh? That's what you think you is, a man?" she said, raising her voice, as if what I said was the most ridiculous thing in the world.

"You *are* a man." I corrected her.

"Stop trying to put words in my mouth, and answer the question."

"You got to be patient with PeeWee. PeeWee is an orphan with nobody to care about him. That's why he does what he does."

"Of course he is, the biggest orphan in the world, to hear him tell it, with two uncles fighting each other to do for him."

"But they don't really care about PeeWee, and you know it. Sure they give him stuff and let him stay at their homes, but that's only because each one is trying to outdo the other. He ain't got no father like you and I."

"Hasn't got a father, like you and me," she said, correcting me. "So that's what you trying to be, now, Pee-Wee's father."

She gave me a sharp look, and I scrambled around in my mind, trying to come up with something else to say. "Look, Dorasthena, just let him come along. I need

PeeWee, need him to help me carry the wreath. Okay?"

I could see that Dorasthena didn't quite believe me. "I can't understand why you need PeeWee so close to you all of a sudden. That wreath ain't all that big. I could carry it myself."

"Well, if that's the way you want it, go right ahead. This whole thing is your idea anyway. Go right ahead."

She wasn't about to go into the cemetery by herself. So she gave me a dirty look like I was taking unfair advantage—which I was. But getting her to change her mind was never easy. The truth is I was desperate; the real reason I wanted PeeWee to go along with us to the cemetery was so that I wouldn't have to be alone with Dorasthena, not for a while. The bus finally came, and we got on.

People looked at us when we got on the bus and headed straight for the backseat. Black people don't care much for the back of the bus since Dr. King and Reverend Abernathy and Mrs. Rosa Parks had the bus boycott in Montgomery. But that was the only seat wide enough to hold the three of us and the big wreath too. So that's where we sat. Nobody talking to anybody.

You see, Dorasthena really is the best friend I ever had. I had already told her I had something serious I wanted to talk to her about. It was about Daddy . . . about how strangely he was behaving since the bombing and what I ought to do about it. But even more, how to explain the children's march in such a way that he couldn't get angry and maybe forbid me to go. The only person I can get that kind of advice from is Dorasthena. She was a good listener. She has a lot of sympathy, but was always trying to hide it by being sarcastic.

But Dorasthena really thought Daddy was crazy. That he should be put away before he hurt somebody. And that made any sensible conversation about my father almost impossible. I needed to figure out just how much to tell her and what to leave out. But I wasn't ready for the kind of talk I needed to have with Dorasthena. So that's why I needed PeeWee to go with us. It would give me time to get my story together.

First was what happened the very night of the bombing. Ike had been swearing all day, mostly to himself. The Edlee brothers had to be involved; they had to be the ones behind it all. And the one black man in town they couldn't intimidate, the only one they were really afraid of, was Isaac Stone. The man they had sworn one day to hunt down and kill. The church was only the beginning. Knowing them he believed they would strike again. And maybe this time, closer to home.

"But one thing they better understand, them Edlee brothers," I heard him saying to himself, ". . . come messing around my house they better shoot straight. Ike Stone is shooting back, and Ike don't miss!" And then he went out to the pickup, got his pistol, brought it back, and put it under his pillow.

I tried to go to sleep but I was scared; but not of the Edlee brothers. Ike had promised Mama Lucy, on her deathbed—she made him swear on the Bible—that under no circumstances would he ever bring his pistol into the house. And I didn't know exactly how something like that—making a promise to somebody dying, and then breaking it—was going to work out. I tossed and turned for the longest time. We slept in different rooms, across the hall from each other.

Later in the night I heard Ike groaning. He was tossing and turning, too, and kept mumbling those same bad words. Finally I heard him throw the covers off and jump out of bed. Then he must have taken the pistol from under his pillow, because I saw him as he passed my door. He was carrying it in his hand. I heard him go outside and into the garage. After a while he came back, this time without it. And we both went to sleep.

But the next night he woke me up again. Something must have been wrong with the phone in the bedroom for him to have to talk as loud as he did.

"No, Phil, this time I mean it. This time I am serious. As soon as I can get some money together and arrange a few things, I'm coming out to California. No, not for a visit. Me and the boy, we're coming out to stay!"

That was what really woke me up in full. Uncle Phil—I'd never met him, except to say hello a time or two on the phone—was one of Daddy's Korean War veteran buddies. The only one he kept in contact with. Even before Mama Lucy died, Uncle Phil had been after Daddy to move his family out to California, where there was plenty of work at good wages for a good carpenter and cabinetmaker like Daddy.

And Daddy was always telling Uncle Phil on the phone, whenever he called, which was about once or twice a month, that he and I were going to leave this "stinking, rotten, racist, Jim Crow town and go out to California," where he and Uncle Phil could go into business together. Sometimes, when things got slow and there wasn't much work for Daddy and his pickup, he talked to me about it. Daddy wasn't much of a talker, like I told you, so when he did talk I knew it was time to listen, and listen good.

Of course the last thing I wanted to do in all this world was to leave Holy Oak Baptist and Stedman Junior High and all my friends, especially, I reckon, Dorasthena, and go to California, or anywhere else. But I was with him that day at the cemetery when he promised Mama Lucy that he would never leave her alone out there, and I know him well enough to know he meant it. So up to now I had never really worried.

But that night, talking on the phone, he scared me. I needed desperately to talk to somebody, to get some advice from somebody, and Dorasthena was the only person I could turn to.

I must have gotten pretty deep into my thoughts,

because suddenly Dorasthena was shaking me by the shoulder. "Stone!" she was saying. Everybody on the bus must have heard her. "You're not listening to a word I say."

"I am so listening." Sometimes it's easier to lie than to argue.

"Oh? You mean that you agree with PeeWee?"

"Agree with PeeWee about what?"

"Forget it." She looked at me with disgust and turned and looked out, with her back to me all the way out to the cemetery.

The sun was still high when we got to the gate. Dorasthena glanced nervously around and back over her shoulder, as if the weather was cold. She hadn't been out here since they buried her grandmother, and even then they had to make her come. I have a sneaking suspicion that Dorasthena must have owed Mollie Mae and Carole a good little piece of money when they died . . . or something strong like that, and that her conscience was bothering her over it, else she probably would have stayed behind at the gate and sent PeeWee and me in with the flowers.

It was quite a walk along the road that ran by the fence until we got to the back, where the new graves were.

"See? Look at that; what did I tell you?" What was left of the funeral flowers were still on the graves—two long mounds of sunburned clay side by side near the back wall—but withered and dried and dead, ready to be hauled away by the caretakers and burned with the rest of the trash. Bits of colored ribbon and green wrapping paper lay scattered about in the yellow dirt. "What a mess."

"They wouldn't have wilted if somebody had come out here and put water on them." PeeWee spoke up, making about as silly a remark as I have ever heard.

The wreath Mrs. Ellis had made up for us was big, built on a circle of wire, and had wooden legs that let it stand up. Trouble was, it was only one wreath and there were two graves.

"Why don't we run back to Mrs. Ellis for another one," PeeWee said, looking at Dorasthena but talking to me, " and leave Dorasthena alone in the graveyard. We might get back before dark if we hurried."

"Shut up, PeeWee, and don't be stupid. You're just trying to make somebody nervous. Just set it down there at the head between the two of them, so it can keep them both company."

We put the wreath where she showed us, then stood for a while without saying anything. The little breeze, blowing in from the river, ruffled the sash with the two names on it. It blew the smell of the flowers in our direction. The whole thing seemed sort of quiet and sad and nice—almost religious. Which is pretty much how all of us in the Young People's Bible Class still feel about the two friends we lost. Good-bye, Mollie Mae. Good-bye, Carole. We sure are going to miss you.

Then we gathered up the old dead flowers and

dumped them behind some bushes. Dorasthena broke off a branch from one of the bushes and made it into a broom. She smoothed out the dirt on top of the graves and swept the space around and between them. Then she sighed with deep satisfaction. "Flowers are nice; but they sure don't last very long."

"There's got to be something we can do, even more than flowers." PeeWee added.

"There is. We are going to have a children's march. Except this fool had to go and run his mouth and make Reverend Cable mad."

"I told you, I am going to beg his pardon," PeeWee said.

"Even if you have to get down on your knees?"

"Even if I have to get down on my knees."

"Then I'll go with him," I said. "I'm the president, and he must be over being mad at us by now. I'm sure he'll let us have a march, if we ask him nice."

"I'm going too," said Dorasthena.

The light from the sun was changing. We hated to leave, but we had to. On the way out the two of them went with me to Mama Lucy's grave and stopped a minute. I would love to have taken Dorasthena by her grandmother's grave, but she didn't remember where it was. "Come on, Dorasthena, we've still got time; maybe we can find it."

"No, no. Let's go. I want to get home before my father does; let's get out of here."

We passed through the gate and went to the bus stop, then turned and looked back. Way across on the other side, on a little rise, near the back wall, we saw the wreath standing between the two graves in the glow of the afternoon sunlight, and thought it was the prettiest thing in the whole place.

7

The next Sunday the Young People's Bible Class was meeting again for the first time since the bombing two weeks before. The interior wall hadn't been touched yet, and the big hole gaped where the bomb had gone off. The whole space was still roped off, piled high with junk and rubble. But across the hall was a small chapel, which was also used sometimes for night school, and Reverend Cable told us to use that until our old classroom was repaired.

We had our Sunday School books opened to the story of Daniel, which was one of my favorites. Deacon Grantham was leading us through the lesson and stopping every so often to explain what was happening to Daniel, as if we didn't already know, having heard him do the same thing in the same way maybe a hundred times—or so it seemed. He was an old man, bent over from being a farmer for so many years. His hair was white and cut close to his skull. Big gray circles around the pupils of his eyes made him look like an owl every time he blinked. The suit he wore was blue, or once had been, and it was shiny in places from being worn so much. His collar was always clean and white and stiff and much too big for his scrawny black neck. His mouth seemed pointed like a barracuda. He chewed on his teeth, and they clicked and whistled as he talked. He was always trying to make the words sound bigger and holier because they had come from the Bible.

I loved the story about Daniel, but not the way Deacon Grantham told it. It made me feel just about as sorry for the lions as I did for Daniel. I had to nudge PeeWee in his side from time to time to keep him from falling asleep. Just as I was about to fall asleep myself, Reverend Cable came bouncing in. Thank the Lord for that. He asked Deacon Grantham to excuse him. He had just got back from seeing Dr. King in Atlanta and there was a lot he had to tell us, but it would only take a minute. Deacon Grantham clicked his teeth and took a seat.

"But first—Pearlicia Cabelle, Rhoda Turner has called in sick. You think you could handle the organ at the eleven o'clock service today in her stead?"

First Pearlicia squealed, like a stuck pig, and then she said, "Oh yes, sir, I don't think so, Reverend Cable, I know so. Oh, Lord have mercy. Excuse me." She clapped her hand over her mouth and almost had a fit, trying to keep her feet still.

"Well, go on upstairs; you'll have to convince Mrs. Ross. She's probably in the choir room. Go over the order of worship and the music and see if you can play it."

Pearlicia jumped up and started out so fast she forgot her pocketbook.

"Take it easy, young lady, don't break your neck. Maybe if I can arrange it we'll be able to give you a few minutes practice before service."

"I don't need that, Reverend Cable. Everything Mrs. Ross and the choir can sing, I can play."

"Oh? Well, excuse me, Miss Thing, but be careful: pride goeth before a fall. First clinker I hear, I'm throwing my hymn book at you." As Pearlicia ran out the door Reverend Cable was laughing, something I hadn't seen on his face in a long time.

"I understand your lesson for today is about Daniel in the lions' den, which is exactly what you young people are going to be facing, come Friday next."

A white newspaper photographer, who looked like a boy with a beard, came through the open door. When Reverend Cable turned to see who it was, he aimed his camera at Reverend Cable's face and a flash went off. He started to back out the door.

"Just a minute, young man." Reverend Cable, still smiling, reached out and snatched the camera away. "In this house, God comes first, not the camera. Now, I'll just hold on to this for you." He set the camera down on the desk in front of him. "Right after church service, we're going to let you take all the pictures you want. Meanwhile, you sit right there; go ahead, make yourself right at home. Members of the Holy Oak Young People's Bible Class, I want you all to say welcome to our young newspaper friend."

We all said "Welcome" in unison. The boy sat down in a great big hurry, and Reverend Cable went right on with the lesson.

"Now, although I didn't get it from Stone, or Dorasthena, I understand you children are planning a march this coming Friday week to honor the memory of your classmates, Mollie Mae and Carole."

"And Hookie Fenster," PeeWee piped up.

"Hookie is still alive; we pray for his full recovery. The children's march is a tribute for them all. Is that right?"

Everybody sort of looked at one another, and then at me and Dorasthena; but nobody said anything.

"Well, when I first heard about it, it made me angry. I thought it was foolish, I thought it was dangerous. And most of all, I didn't appreciate not being told about what's going on in my church, right behind my back, by young people I thought I could trust and depend on. People I called the leaders of tomorrow."

We all sat there, not looking at Reverend Cable, but squirming down into our seats. Nobody said anything until PeeWee stood up and spoke again: "I was in on it too. It was my fault for not telling you first, Reverend Cable, and I'm sorry. I promise never to do a thing like that again." He looked straight at Dorasthena, then sat back down.

"Yes, bless your heart, PeeWee, indeed you were. Now, as I said, I was so angry that I was prepared to forbid you to march, to tell you no! But when I told Martin about this foolish, dangerous, and awful thing you had done, he was so touched, he just sat there for a moment almost on the verge of tears. He thought it was wonderful. So, I was wrong, and I apologize. . . . Apologize, because, unlike Daniel, I didn't have the faith I am always preaching in the pulpit . . . the faith that God would see us through, just as he did Daniel in the lions' den. Martin says if you children want to march, go right ahead. He is behind you one hundred percent . . . that he will be glad to come and lead the march. We grown-ups have a duty, not only to let you march, but also to pitch in and help in every way we can. So, congratulations, class, from Martin, and from me."

PeeWee jumped to his feet again, and started to clap, and so did the rest of us. The photographer stood up, too, but he didn't clap.

"Okay, okay. I want all of you to meet with me in my

office just before the morning service. So we can have something to announce to the congregation—and to the world. Thank you, Deacon Grantham."

He scooped up the camera from the desk and started off. "And by the way, Martin said we've got to have permission, written permission from your parents, so don't forget." The photographer had to run to keep up with Reverend Cable's long-legged walk.

When they heard about it, the congregation rose to its feet and applauded, long and loud. A whole lot of people said Amen! and some said Hallelujah! Mollie Mae's father got up after they quieted down, and it took him a minute to stand up straight, clear his throat, and blow his nose. He said how hard it was for him and his wife, having lost their only child; but he just had to rise and express the family's heartfelt thanks and gratitude—especially to the Young People's Bible Class.

Then Carole's father got up. He looked at the ceiling, then down to the floor. "And a little child shall lead them." That's all he said; then he sat back down.

"Just what we needed," said Big Mother. It was after the benediction and she was on her way down to the kitchen. She grabbed me and gave me a big hug. "Praise God! Those darling girls will not have died in vain. And did you hear Pearlicia, playing up there? . . . Made that ol' organ holler." She squeezed my hand and kissed me on the cheek and whispered, "Come downstairs, I saved you and Ike a whole half a chicken."

After service people gathered downstairs to eat and to socialize. Nobody seemed to want to leave. They'd rather stay and talk, mostly about the march. Meanwhile we met in Reverend Cable's office and had our picture taken.

Of course it was no excuse, but I hadn't had the time to sit down with Dorasthena and figure out a way to make sure Daddy would let me march. There were a thousand things that had to be done now that the march was official. I got so busy that it was easy to keep putting it off. I would die if he wouldn't let me march. I knew had to tell him, but I didn't know how. Then all of a sudden Daddy took the whole thing right out of my hands. Instead of me telling him, he told me.

"Son . . ." that was the way it started. He was driving me to school, and we had about ten more blocks to go, and it was already 8:30. He pulled the pickup over to the side of the road and stopped and turned off the motor. "You and me, we need to talk."

"Yes, sir. Talk about what, sir?"

"Talk is all over town about this children's march. Everywhere I go, black folks—and white folks—all talking about it. I been waiting ever since I first heard for you to come to me and tell me about it, but you didn't. You didn't say a word. I wondered why."

"I'm sorry, Daddy. I know I should have told you. But—but—"

"But you were scared, right? Right?"

I had to think a moment. I hadn't thought about it before, but honestly, I had to tell him yes.

He looked up the road awhile before he spoke. "My son, my own flesh and blood, not scared of the sheriff and his deputies with their billy clubs; of the police with their dogs and water hoses; marching in the streets with people screaming and cussing and throwing things—not scared of that, but scared to death of his own father. I wonder what Lucy would say to me about that." He sighed hard, and looked up the road again.

"This children's march thing is like a red flag to a bull. And you right there in the middle of it. That's hard, mighty hard, for me to swallow. I said to myself that I was going to tell you no. But I couldn't. I asked myself, over and over again: What would Lucy do if she was here? That wasn't the answer either. So you and me, we got to settle this whole nonviolent thing—man to man—once and for all. And we got to settle it now."

What did he mean by that? I had taken a vow to be nonviolent just like Dr. King. What would I do if Daddy ordered me to change my mind?

"You ain't but almost fourteen, but that don't mean you still a baby. You old enough to have your own way of doing things, even if it is nonviolent—which certainly ain't my way. I think it's wrong; I think it's weak; I think it's for cowards and sissies. It's already got them two girls killed. I mean, if I was to say to you right now, I admire what you all are trying to do, but you stay home, not get mixed up in it. Would you do it?"

"I wouldn't want to disobey you, Daddy."

"Dammit, son. This ain't baby talk. If I asked you, man to man, not to get mixed up in this children's march, what would you say? What would you do?"

"Man to man?"

"Yeah, man to man."

"I'd tell you how sorry I was, and then I think . . . I'd go. I think I'd have to."

"Even though you might get hurt or even killed, you'd still have to go?"

"Yes, sir." That was all I could say.

"Well, like I said . . . a man has got to do what he's got to do."

My daddy was calling me a man. I couldn't believe it!

"You got your way, and I got mine. You children will be putting yourselves in harm's way, and since I can't stop you, I'll have to go with you."

"What's that, sir?"

"I said, I'll have to go with you."

* * *

A couple of days later we sat side by side in Miss Redmond's arithmetic class. Miss Redmond was very strict and didn't stand for nobody—for anybody—talking in her class. I would have to wait till the lunch recess before I could tell Dorasthena about my father.

But just before the bell, Professor Duckett sent word he wanted to see me in his office right away. I asked Dorasthena to go to our special bench behind the gym where we usually had lunch and wait. I had some special news to tell her, and I wouldn't be long. This was Thursday. Tomorrow the march would take place. There were still a lot of things to do, and that was what I thought the principal wanted to see me about.

But Professor Duckett wasn't in his office. I waited for him awhile and then I left. I ran to my locker, took my lunch from my book bag, and went to the spot where we usually had lunch—if somebody didn't beat us to it first. Dorasthena gave me half her bacon and egg sandwich, and I gave her half my tuna.

"You said you wanted to talk to me," Dorasthena said, taking a big bite. "So talk."

"You said that Daddy wasn't going to let me be in the children's march, didn't you? Well, you were wrong."

"What you mean?"

"I mean on my way to school this morning, he stopped the truck and we sat and had a long talk, just him and me, man to man. He said I could go."

"How do I know you're not telling a lie?" she said.

"On Mama Lucy's grave, I'm telling the truth." Dorasthena stopped chewing and looked at me real hard. "Right there, on Oakley Street, that's where we parked. That's why I was late this morning. He said he was sorry he didn't let me go on the bus to Washington. And what is more, Daddy's coming to the march too."

Dorasthena stood up in such a hurry, the tuna sandwich fell to the ground. "Coming to the march? Why?"

"What do you mean, why? The same reason I'm coming, and you and everybody else: to show the world we are not afraid. That's why he's coming to the march."

"But we can't let your father be in the children's march, Stone. He'll bring his pistol!"

"Bring his pistol for what?"

"In case any of them white people get in his way or do anything that he doesn't like, he'll pull out his pistol and shoot 'em!"

"That's crazy, Dorasthena, that is absolutely crazy."

"Why else would somebody as crazy as your father come to the march, except to shoot somebody, you tell me that!"

I hate to say this, but at that moment, if I hadn't been nonviolent, I would have popped her in her mouth. Instead of praising my father for what he was doing, she kept telling me how crazy he was. So I just gritted my teeth and walked away without another word.

I went back to Professor Duckett's office. He was in this time and introduced me to a stout man with a lot of bulging muscles and a face I had seen a hundred times in the big photograph on the wall behind the desk. "Stone, this is Mutts Malone, an old friend of Lucy's and your father's. He's assistant athletic director over at Morehouse now, and he wants to talk to you about football." They sat me down, and that's exactly what they did, the both of them, for almost an hour; but football was the last thing on my mind.

Daddy was busy doing a job down in Columbiana and wouldn't be home till late that night, so I had supper by myself, fixed his plate, and left it in the oven.

Then I rushed to finish my homework so that I could rehearse. Dr. King had sent us a letter saying that he would be glad to come and lead the children's march. I wanted to be perfect—to sound exactly like him—so he could be proud.

I brushed my teeth, got into my pajamas, said my prayers, then crawled into bed. I propped myself up with the pillows and said those beautiful words over and over. But underneath, in spite of myself, my mind kept drifting away from the words and on to Dorasthena. I finally decided I was through being Dorasthena's friend, and after the march I would tell her so.

And then I must have fell—fallen—asleep, because the next thing I knew, there I was playing football with Mama Lucy in what looked to me like a great big rose garden that smelled just like her perfume. Neither of us had any shoes on, and she kept yelling to me, "Watch out, honey. Be careful, don't step on the thorns; and whatever you do, don't tell Ike." I was crashing through the roses trying to catch the ball she threw at me. I fell down, but I caught the ball, and she ran to see if I was hurt and to pick me up. But I'm a big boy now, and I was too heavy. So we just sat, with her kneeling down behind me, and me leaning back in her arms. She hugged me, and tickled me, and we were laughing and laughing and laughing.

Then she stopped laughing and looked very serious and a little sad as she bent over me. "Listen, Stone," she whispered, "there is something I want to tell you about your father, but you mustn't tell him I told you." I promised not to, but what she told me woke me straight up, and I sat there, still smelling her perfume, even if she wasn't there any longer. And the first thing I said to myself was: "Dorasthena is right about the pistol, Mama." And just like that, I knew what I had to do.

I didn't know how late it had got. Across the hall I could hear Daddy snoring in the bedroom, kind of soft and easy. He must have come home while I was asleep and got his supper and gone to bed. We had a big clock on the mantelpiece in the sitting room that belonged to Mama Lucy's grandfather. We kept the clock wound up and running even if it didn't tell the right time anymore. It would strike at all kinds of crazy times in the day or the night. It never had bothered me before, but tonight I could hear it ticking. It struck two times. I got up, got on my knees beside the bed, and said my prayers for the second time that night. That gave me courage and made me feel better.

The clock was ticking so loud that I was surprised it didn't wake up Daddy. I put on my bedroom slippers, stuck my head into his room, and stood there a minute, listening. It was too dark to see, but I could tell from his breathing that he was sound asleep. I tiptoed through the hall, through the kitchen, where I picked up the flashlight, and out onto the back porch. Then I went down the steps and out into the garage.

I climbed up into the seat of the pickup and tried to open the glove compartment where Daddy kept his pistol, but it was locked. I sat there for a minute. I couldn't give up; I promised Mama Lucy in the dream that I would take care of it. Take care of everything. I had to get the keys to open the compartment. And there was but one way to do that: sneak into Daddy's room and take them out of his pocket.

I tiptoed back into the house and eased down the hall. I stood outside the door to Daddy's room and listened. He was still asleep. I knew where he kept his keys: they were in his pants, which he always kept on a chair at the foot of his bed. You been in a room a thousand times, so you think you know it by heart—where every piece of furniture is, so that you can move around in the dark without bumping into things.

But suppose the rocking chair wasn't by the wall, but rather next to the window . . . suppose he woke up while I was in there and mistook me for a burglar. All these things kept running through my head. But I thought of the promise I had made to Mama Lucy. So I shut my eyes a minute and asked the Lord to make me as brave as I could get, then tiptoed into the room, and got the keys, and came back without making a single sound. I moved so fast it scared me. And Daddy didn't move a muscle.

I went back to the garage, opened the glove compartment, and pulled the pistol out. Just then a scratching sound in the corner made me jump. I swung the light around till it hit two shiny brown eyes as bright as fire staring up at me. It was either a possum or a coon or maybe even a polecat that had crawled in through a small hole in the back wall of the garage. The eyes blinked once or twice and then went out like a light. Whatever it was had disappeared. I ran back to the porch, opened the door to the kitchen, and then, looking down the hall, I saw Daddy's shadow coming in my direction! If he came into the kitchen he would catch me for sure.

I waited, frozen there in the doorway, the pistol in one hand, the flashlight in the other, not daring even to breathe, until I heard the toilet flush, and then his feet padding back. I heard the springs creak and soon he was snoring, nice and loud again. I counted to a hundred just to make sure, then I went to my room and put the pistol in the safest place I could think of: under my own pillow. Then I tiptoed into Daddy's room again and put the keys back in his pocket. I must have been holding my breath, 'cause it felt just like when I run three laps around the cinder path.

And then, feeling very happy with myself, I hopped into my bed, crawled under the covers, and soon was fast asleep.

8

It was a perfect day for a march. Daddy had awak-ened me at 4:00 A.M. to tell me he was leaving for the job. Columbiana was a long way, but he would be sure to be back in time, and not to worry. No matter what happened, he would be there to protect me.

I didn't say a word. After he left the room, I lay there in bed afraid to move. What if he looked in the glove compartment and found his pistol gone? He would know it was me—I. I was the only person who knew where he kept it. But after what seemed like forever, I heard the motor start up, and the pickup pulling out, then it was gone. But his leaving must have waked all the birds in the neighborhood. There they were, busy making early morning noises in the chinaberry tree behind the garage. Then they left, too, just as sudden. Then it was still and quiet and peaceful everywhere as I lay there, going over the details of how the march was to take place.

The Young People's Bible Class, led by Dr. King and Reverend Cable, would step off from Holy Oak Baptist at 10:00 A.M. and march through the streets to Stedman Junior High Stadium, which was only about a mile away. At the same time, teachers from all over town would march at the heads of their classes to Stedman, also. Meanwhile parents and friends and family, together with the newspaper people with their cameras, would gather at the stadium and wait. It was going to be very, very simple. I thought about Mama Lucy again, the dream I had had, and said to myself: "Yes, a perfect day for the march."

I got so caught up in practicing in front of the mirror I missed the first bus and had to wait for the second. Dorasthena was already there, waiting at the door. "Why did you bring your book bag?" In some ways Dorasthena can be the nosiest person in the world. But this morning, I was determined not to be angry with her, or with anybody else, so I just ignored the question.

"Where is everybody?"

"Downstairs in Reverend Cable's office arguing."

"Arguing? Good!"

Dorasthena was much more concerned with talking than with listening; she probably didn't hear me.

"Reverend Cable went to Atlanta to get Dr. King,

and he isn't back yet, so you got to be the one to handle it."

"Handle what?" I said, not stopping to talk but going on about my business, leaving her with her mouth open, staring at my back, which made me feel just great.

But downstairs Billy Cabelle was waiting at the foot of the steps, and I could tell by the way he looked that whatever was wrong, it was big. Billy Cabelle was the quietest member of the class. That was because he stuttered and was afraid that the rest of us would make fun. He seldom spoke at all, let alone raised his voice. But now he was shaking all over from trying to speak and not being able to.

"Sto-Sto-Sto . . ." He kept trying, but that's as far as he got.

"What's wrong, Billy, what's the matter? What are you trying to say?"

"Don't ask him, ask your friend PeeWee. It's his mess."

"Oh, for Pete's sake, Dorasthena, Billy can speak for himself."

But Billy couldn't speak for himself. I looked around for Pearlicia. Usually when Billy was in a hurry, he'd point to Pearlicia, and she'd finish his sentences for him. But she wasn't there.

"Reverend Cable isn't back from Atlanta yet, so you got to be the one to handle it."

"Please, Dorasthena, I'm trying to talk to Billy, so will you please shut up!" I had never spoken to her like that before. She gave me a look that was awful, then turned and left us alone.

"What is it, Billy, what are you trying to say?" He shook his head as hard as he could, trying to force the words out; but nothing came. "Take it easy, Billy, take it easy." I took him by the arm and headed toward Reverend Cable's office.

Downstairs in the rec room some of the same television and newspaper people from before were having coffee and homemade doughnuts made by Big Mother herself. The smell of bacon and ham was coming from the kitchen, where Big Mother would be busy doing what she always did whenever something big was going on at Holy Oak—complaining and mumbling to herself about this being the very last time. Cooking grits and scrambling eggs and cooking other stuff, which nobody had asked her to cook in the first place.

The whole Young People's Bible Class was crowded into Reverend Cable's office. We had decided to march in our ushers' uniforms, which as I told you, were white. Mrs. Ellis was trying to pin on the white roses she had donated just for the occasion. It was hard to get anybody to stand still or be quiet, because everybody was angry and talking about PeeWee.

"Stone!" Billy Cabelle finally managed and looked at PeeWee—but that was as far as he could make it. He twisted his face, beat his hands on his thighs, then sat down, gave up and looked at the floor, and pointed at Dorasthena.

But Roscoe Malone beat her to the punch. "You better tell this Uncle Tom fool something, Stone," he said, looking at PeeWee.

"I ain't no Uncle Tom, no such thing." Knowing that I would protect him, PeeWee all of a sudden got brave and loud. He tried to move to where I was but Mrs. Ellis was hanging on to his lapels.

"Hold still, PeeWee, before you make me stick this pin in you, boy!"

"Tell him what? What has PeeWee done that everybody is so angry about?"

"PeeWee called Mrs. Tucker Stribling on the phone and invited her to come and lead the march." Roscoe Malone was steaming.

"What!"

"In the first place, Dr. King is going to lead the march—him and Reverend Cable. They're the only grown-ups from the church that we're going to let do any leading. Okay?" I looked at PeeWee to make sure he got the point.

"But it's already ten thirty. Suppose they don't get back in time," PeeWee said.

"Then we'll wait until they do get back. Right, Stone?" Roscoe answered back.

"We can't wait. I'm the grand marshall. We're supposed to be there at Stedman Stadium before the children from the other schools arrive. I'm supposed to show them where to go."

"If Reverend Cable and Dr. King don't get here in time, that white lady will be leading the march," Thelma Dodd called out from across the room.

"And if she's leading the march, then I ain't marching," Roscoe said, and started to take off his coat.

"Watch what you're doing, Roscoe, you're smashing my nicest flower." Mrs. Ellis was having a time.

Billy Cabelle made funny noises, like he was choking, then pointed to Dorasthena.

"I ain't marching either," she said, looking around. "Them white folks want to march, let them do it themselves. I sure ain't going." The others nodded their heads, grumbling their agreement. Then everybody looked at me.

"All right, Stone, you're the president," Roscoe said. "So what are we supposed to do?"

All I could think of was I still hadn't had a chance to get to the utility room and hide the pistol I was carrying in my book bag, so I wasn't really listening to any of them. But before I could speak Pearlicia came rushing in. "She's here. Her and that ol' man she calls her secretary, driving up in that ol' white hearse," she said, and started back.

"It ain't no hearse, it's a Rolls-Royce," Dorasthena said, running off after her. Everybody else was distracted. It gave me my chance. I ducked out, ran to the utility room, stashed my book bag under the choir robes, then hurried back.

Mr. Purdy came in sweating and with a smile that didn't quite fit. "Mrs. Tucker Stribling is sitting outside in the car. She'd like to see Reverend Cable."

"Tell him, Stone." Dorasthena said. Everybody turned and looked as she came and stood at my side.

"Reverend Cable went to Atlanta to pick up Dr. King. They didn't get here yet. Can I help you? I'm Junior Assistant Pastor."

"Well, she just wanted him to know that she appreciated the invitation; but her arthritis is acting up. She won't be able to march with you children after all. We'll just follow along in the car."

Just at that moment Reverend Cable came hurrying into the office, pulling off his coat, getting into his robe, and having his flower pinned on. "Martin is still in jail in Albany. We'll have to proceed without him. But here's a message, Stone, he wants you to read to the rally. And he sends love."

Reverend Cable looked at me. He knew how hard I had been practicing, and how much I had been looking forward to having Dr. King hear me recite his famous speech. Then he went on.

"Now, children, you remember what you've been taught. Be on the alert. Keep your eyes open at all times. Watch out for people who throw things; duck if you have to. If you are attacked and cannot escape, drop to the ground and curl up in a knot, elbows over your face, and keep your head covered with your arms. Got that?"

"Yes, sir," everybody answered.

"And whatever you do, if anybody hits you, you mustn't hit back. That's what nonviolence means. There's still time for anybody who wants to to change their mind—"

"No, sir." Nobody was about to change their mind.

And then he looked at me again. "Sorry, Stone."

True, I was disappointed, but I didn't mind so much; after all Daddy would be there and he would hear me. And that would make the whole thing even better. So I took Dr. King's telegram, and looked Reverend Cable straight in the eye, and gave him a great big smile. I almost started to wink. And he smiled too. A perfect day for a march indeed.

The television people were waiting for us on the sidewalk across the street. Their microphones were pointed in people's faces, and flashbulbs were popping all over the place. A crowd of neighborhood folks had gathered, and when they saw us thirteen children, dressed in our ushers' whites with white roses in our lapels in honor of Hookie Fenster and our dead class-mates, they started to applaud. But the march was sup-posed to be silent, like the one the NAACP had back in 1917, so we didn't respond at all, didn't say a word.

Reverend Cable, looking straight ahead, stepped out into the middle of the street. We stepped out behind him. And we were off. The march was underway.

Other people had gathered in the street. They called or waved to us as we passed, but we didn't say a word. At first it was mostly black people; but the closer we got to the school, the more white people came out to watch us pass. The black people cheered and said how nice we looked and how proud they were of us for what we were doing. The white people mostly stood stiff and silent. And most of them looked angry, and some of them, mean.

The combined choirs from Holy Oak and some of the deacons and trustees and other members, led by Deacon Grantham, followed us, and behind them, bringing up the rear, Mrs. Tucker Stribling's white Rolls-Royce came chugging along. Mr. Purdy was driving, while she and Mr. Mac McIllister were sitting in the back.

I marched in the center, right behind Reverend Cable with Dorasthena at my right and PeeWee, strutting like a peacock, at my left. I halfway wondered if maybe I should close my eyes a little as we marched, so I could go over the I Have a Dream speech one more time in my head. Now that Dr. King couldn't be there it was up to me to do what he would do, and say what he would say. I was determined to make it sound as much like him as I could.

Things had been mostly quiet up till now, but as we turned into Ridgely Street, which is only three blocks from the school, the crowd on the sidewalk was mostly white and was beginning to sound different. Somebody shouted "Nigger," not once but several times. It was starting to get scary. This was no time to think about closing my eyes. What I did think about was how to keep being nonviolent, like Reverend Cable had taught us, in case anything was to happen. The main thing about nonviolence, I said to myself — no matter what happens — is not to be afraid.

The crowd got even bigger and more noisy. Policemen, dressed in riot gear and carrying long, mean-looking billy clubs, were standing in a line about twenty feet apart between us and the crowd that jammed the sidewalk. They stared at us with mean and hateful eyes. I was more afraid of them than I was of the people, who by now were shouting, waving their fists, cursing, and calling out: "Martin Luther Coon" and "Go Back to Africa!" — all sorts of nasty names. One man I saw, standing right next to a policeman, looked to me like one of the Edlee Brothers — the one who had been on television. But I wasn't sure.

We passed a big red fire truck parked at the fire hydrant, with the hoses already hooked up. Farther up the street was the paddy wagon, which everybody called the Black Mariah, standing there with its doors wide open. It had bars on the windows, and a big padlock on the back door, and was used for hauling people off to jail. Next to it were four big men from the sheriff's office, each holding a giant hungry-looking snarling slobbering police dog on a leash. The dogs had the longest, sharpest, ugliest teeth I ever saw. The sun was high; we were right in the middle of the heat of the day. But in spite of that I was shivering so much I felt my teeth clacking. But I wasn't cold. I wasn't exactly scared either—I don't know what I was.

Just before we turned into the school yard I saw a deputy sheriff snatch a camera from a newspaperman and smash it to the pavement, then stomp on it. We were late. The stadium was already almost full and some of the schools were still marching through the gate and getting into place. We had to wait and let them go in first.

We finally did march through, and the first thing I saw, standing in the crowd, was my father. I was so busy thinking about the speech, I had forgotten about taking his pistol. Maybe that's why it was such a shock all of a sudden to see him there, looking straight at me, and mad enough to bite somebody.

I fully expected him to reach over, pull me from the line, and beat my butt right then and there in front of everybody. I couldn't have blamed him. But he didn't move—didn't move an inch, just stood there looking dead at me. I knew from that look that when he got me home I was in trouble. But then I thought of Mama Lucy, and I felt better. This was between me and her.

No matter what Daddy did to me I knew that I was right. Not because I'm a coward, but because it was the nonviolent thing do to.

The rest of what happened that day went by so fast everything is a blur from beginning to end. But this—to the best of my recollection—is how I think the whole thing went.

PeeWee moved people out of the way so our class could stand right in front of the platform, then Reverend Cable and I went up the steps. On one corner was the piano, with Pearlicia sitting there. Professor Duckett, and Carole's mother and father, and Mollie Mae's mother and father sat in some folding chairs in a row at the back. I looked out over the crowd trying to spot Daddy, but I didn't see him anywhere, almost as if he had suddenly disappeared. Pearlicia played the national anthem, and then the Negro national anthem, which the Stedman Junior High glee club helped everybody to sing.

During all this I kept looking around trying to locate Daddy. But I didn't see him and that worried me so much that I don't remember hearing Reverend Cable give the invocation. The first thing I knew, there I was standing in front of the microphone with the message from Dr. King in my hand, which I heard myself reading:

". . . but I want, first of all, on behalf of the Southern Christian Leadership Conference, and the entire Civil

Rights movement, and most especially myself, to con-
gratulate the Young People's Bible Class of Holy Oak
Baptist Church, who, in the spirit of Christian love and
nonviolence, are today bearing witness to the oldest,
most basic truth of all here in America, that all God's
children, regardless of race, sex, creed, or color, were
indeed, created equal, and endowed by their creator
with . . ."

I was beginning to listen to what was coming out of
the big loudspeakers: my own voice sounding, in my
own opinion, just like Dr. King, and that made me feel
good. I forgot about Daddy, and got myself set to see if
I could do even better, but that's as far as I got. A hand
reached in from behind and snatched the microphone
away. It was the sheriff, who was wearing some big
black sunglasses, so you couldn't really see his eyes.

"The size of the gathering here at this rally," he said,
speaking into the microphone, "has got out of hand, to
such a point it's creating a danger to the public safety.
So I'm going to have to ask all of you-all to disperse
immediately, to leave the area, and return to your
homes."

"But wait a minute, sheriff," said Reverend Cable,
reaching for the microphone, but the sheriff paid him
no mind.

"Anybody who refuses to move, or in any way does
not obey my orders, will be subject to arrest. Now you
got ten minutes to clear the area."

Reverend Cable snatched the microphone away from the sheriff. "Listen, listen, everybody—we have a permit for this march, and to hold this rally; we have a legal right."

The sheriff grabbed Reverend Cable and dragged him across the platform and pushed him down the steps. Then—almost like it was planned—everything went wild. The police, as if they had just been waiting for the signal, moved in and started to swing their clubs at everybody.

I ran over to Reverend Cable to see if he was hurt, but somebody, one of the sheriff's men, picked me up, raised me over his head, and threw me down onto the crowd. Lucky for me I landed against somebody's chest, who caught me, and set my feet on the ground. But before I could steady myself, I was bumped from behind and knocked to my knees. I bent low to the ground, put my chin between my knees and my hand over my head to shield my skull, like Reverend Cable had taught us to do. But then I heard Daddy's voice from somewhere close by calling my name. I managed to raise my head, and to look around, until I saw him pop up from a crowd of people. He was looking at me, pushing people out of the way, trying to move in my direction, but a large red-faced policeman grabbed him from behind.

"Daddy, Daddy!" Everybody else was screaming, and although he was only a few feet away, I found myself screaming too. He broke free, grabbed the stick from the red-faced policeman, and started fighting back. I was all tangled up in somebody's legs, but I managed after a while to get to my feet. I called to him again and moved a few steps in his direction, but the policeman pulled out his pistol and hit Daddy across the head, knocking him down.

"Daddy, Daddy!" Before I could move, somebody knocked me over again, and I found myself on the ground with somebody's knee in my face. I pulled myself into a tight ball and knelt down hugging my knees again. I could hear the sound of people being hit and grunting each time. Twice I felt somebody fall across my back and then slide off.

I don't know how long it took, but after a while the weight was no longer there; nobody was holding me down, so I sneaked my head up a little and looked around. I saw the policeman still hitting my daddy with his pistol butt, and trying to hold him, while two other policemen beat him also, as he struggled to keep them from dragging him away. I stood up, and he saw me. We called out to each other, and tried to reach each other. Then a lot of bodies moved in front of me and I lost sight of what they were doing to Daddy. Somebody grabbed me from behind and held me so that I couldn't move; but I could hear him, even above all that noise, still calling my name.

9

Reverend Cable was talking under his breath as we followed the guard back to the cell where Daddy was. The jailhouse stunk—stank—it had a funny smell, like sick folks. The section at the back, where they kept the colored, was the worst of all. There wasn't much light in the cell, so it wasn't easy to tell it was him, sitting there on a stool bare from the waist up, his head bowed down, like he was looking at his feet, which didn't have any shoes or socks on. There was only a little bulb directly over his head with just enough light to make his black skin shine, especially the shoulders and the arms, which looked as big and as long and as packed full of muscles as ever. I couldn't see his hands, which hung down in the shadow of his lap.

"Isaac, it's me. I brought your son. We've come to take you home."

Daddy didn't move or say anything, so I thought maybe he didn't hear us, but finally he sighed, and grunted, then raised his head. When I saw what they had done to his face, I wanted to run to him and hug him tight and tell him how much I loved him. But the bars were between us. Anyway, I didn't know if he would speak to me after what I had done to him.

"Isaac, you hear me? Are you all right?" Reverend Cable asked.

One eye was swollen shut, the other almost, but I could see there still was anger in it. A deep, raw gash was in his eyebrow, and another one above his left temple. His lips were puffed and busted open at the corner of his mouth. He looked long and hard at Reverend Cable, but not at me. Like I wasn't there. He sucked breath and mumbled something that sounded like a curse; trying to talk must have hurt. Spit, with blood in it, rose over his bottom lip, and dribbled down his chin. He wiped it off with the back of his hand, then dropped his head, and looked at the floor again.

The guard came up behind us and opened the door with a key. "All right, boy, you can go." He left, and we stood there waiting, but Daddy just sat, not moving at all. After a while we went in to see if, maybe, he needed help. Reverend Cable went around behind, put his hands under Daddy's armpits and tried to lift him.

Daddy grunted again—it was more like a growl. He pushed Reverend Cable's hands away, then stood up slow and heavy, wobbling on his feet. And almost fell.

"I'd rather be dead," he said. His lips were so thick and stiff it was hard to understand him. "This ain't no way to treat a man. I'd rather be dead."

"I know, Ike, and if you'd had your pistol out there, you would be. Here, sit back down." But Daddy refused to sit.

"Where's my shoes? I'm getting out of here."

I found his socks, balled up and bloody, wrapped up in his shirt which was covered with blood, dirt, grass stains, and vomit. I think he had used them to try and stop the bleeding. I looked around but I didn't see any shoes.

"Maybe we should send across the square to the haberdashery and buy you something to wear," Reverend Cable said.

"No, I'm leaving now, just like I am." He took a step, but stumbled back onto the stool and sat back down. "Buford Leggitt was the one who brought me down, but he couldn't've done it if it was just me and him. Rest of the police, they ganged up on me, knocked me down with them billy clubs, kicked me in the ribs, in the gut, and in the face. They couldn't've done it, if I had had my pistol."

"No, certainly not—not if you'd had your pistol. Try to stand up again."

Holding his ribs with one hand, he pushed up off the

stool with the other, then slowly, he stood up straight. "This damn fool boy—" he looked at me for the first time, and he made the word sound awful—"went into my truck and stole my pistol. I didn't have a chance."

"I didn't steal it, Daddy. I took it. But I—"

"He's already told me what happened. He took it, Ike, so you couldn't get it, and that's what saved your life."

"This is between me and my boy, Cable, you keep out of it."

"I know it was wrong, Daddy, and I'm sorry."

"Shut up, boy. And what did you do with it? Tell me, before I break your dad-blasted neck!"

"I hid it."

"Hid it where?"

"At the church, downstairs in the utility room, under a pile of choir robes."

"He told me what he had done, and where he put it. I took it, and moved it. It's in my desk now."

"I want it back."

"All right. You'll get it back. But I still say, if this child hadn't done what he did, you'd be dead."

"I'd rather be dead than be treated like I was a nigger. I want my gun back, and I want it back now!"

He stumbled toward the door, but Reverend Cable had to catch him by the arm to keep him from falling. He stood a minute, sweating, trying to get his breath. Slowly unbending, he straightened up again, and then walked straight out, barefoot, his head up, and with no shirt, his arms and back gleaming with sweat as if they had been oiled.

A lot of cars were in the lot when we got to Holy Oak. John Fenster had driven the pickup from the police pound and parked it in the spot where Daddy always waited for me every Sunday. Doc Wheeler came out to meet us and to help get Daddy out of the car. He wanted to take a look at how bad—how badly—he was hurt.

"Where's your shoes, Ike Stone? What are you doing barefoot?"

Daddy gave a grunt, then hobbled on his own toward the door. When he got there he had to stop and lean against it, breathing hard.

"Couldn't find his shoes, Doc Wheeler, and his shirt and socks are a mess," Reverend Cable said as he got out and came around the other side. "Take him down to my office."

"Yes, let's get him inside so I can take a look." Both men had to help Daddy slowly through the door. Mrs. Rhettis came to meet us.

"Reverend Cable," she said, then she saw Daddy's face. It stopped her, but only for a moment. "Dr. King's been trying to reach you. Phoned twice this morning. Said he'd call back. Mr. McIllister is still here, but Mrs. Tucker Stribling had to leave."

"Thank you, Mrs. Rhettis. Would you look upstairs

in the closet in my study? See if you can find a shirt and some socks that Ike can wear. And maybe in the charity box you'll find some shoes and pants."

Mr. McIllister came out of the office, more excited and out of breath than usual. "You hear that, Ike? Mrs. Tucker Stribling is suing the city, and she's just retained me as counsel! She's the one who paid your fine this morning." He looked at Daddy's face. "Oh, my good Lord!"

"Take him into my office, Doc," Reverend Cable said, leading the way.

"All right, all right. But these cuts are going to take some stitches." He started moving Daddy down the hall.

"Where you going, Wheeler? That's not the office. Where are you taking Isaac?"

"The washroom, so I can clean him up a little. His face is a mess."

"Hold on a minute, I need some pictures. Bring him in here, where the light is better," Mr. McIllister said. They took Daddy into the office and sat him down in a chair. Mr. McIllister took the shade off the desk lamp and set it closer, then searched around in his briefcase, which was old and stuffed with papers. The leather was cracking and looked as if it was coming apart. The camera he found was the kind where you can see the picture a minute or two after you take it. "Hold still, Ike, this'll only take a minute."

Nobody hates being fussed over more than my

daddy. "What is this all about, McIllister? What're you taking pictures of me for?"

"It's about evidence. What we need in our suit against the city."

Later, Doc Wheeler took Daddy into the bathroom and washed the dried blood off his face and shoulders. He brought him back into the office and sat him down, then slowly and carefully he started the stitches.

"Will you hurry it up for God's sake? I haven't got all day." Doc Wheeler didn't bother to answer Daddy. He was so busy he didn't even light his cigar.

"What were you saying about Mrs. Tucker Stribling?" Reverend Cable was fishing for something in his desk.

"She's the first white client I ever had. And I thanked her for it. It's quite an honor. The sheriff made her pull her car out of the parade just after we left the church—took the keys and left the two of us sitting there in the back of her Rolls-Royce. Now she wants to sue him for harassment. 'But you know as well as I do,' I told her, 'that suing the sheriff, especially with me as your lawyer, is pretty much a waste of time.' 'It's not a waste of time. It violates my First Amendment rights.' That's what she said. 'The law is a two way street. The Constitution belongs as much to me as it does to the police, but it only works if you make it.' "

Mr. Fenster stuck his head in the door. "Mrs. Rhettis told me to tell you she can't find any clothes to fit him. And the people from the newspapers are here."

"Thank you, John, tell them I'll be right up." Reverend Cable turned to my father. "I'll go up first, but I'm sure they'll want to talk to you, Ike."

"Not me. I ain't got a thing to say to them white folks—not a thing. Ow! Watch it, Doc!"

"For heaven's sake, Ike, sit yourself back down and hold still. I ain't half finished yet."

"I'm just here to get my property, Cable, and that's all," Daddy said.

Reverend Cable started to answer but looked around and changed his mind. "I'll be right back." He locked the desk drawer and went upstairs.

"We'll keep these stitches in for a week or ten days, and then we'll take them out." Doc Wheeler put his needle and thread away, then started to put a bandage on Daddy's head.

"Do you have to put that stuff on me?"

"I know you're a tough man, Ike Stone, but these lacerations are deep, and we don't want them infected, so we got to keep them covered. And keep your seat. I didn't give you your tetanus shot yet."

Doc went back into his bag, and Mr. McIllister kept right on talking: "I was surprised, her being white, that that was something she could understand. And she's right. That's it exactly. Make them live up to their own Constitution."

"Yes, you do that, Mr. Mac. Make them white folks live up to their Constitution. Keep right on dreaming," Daddy said.

"You remember which one of the police it was that hit you?"

"Buford Leggitt. There was others who held me down, but Buford, and his night stick and pistol butt—that's who did it."

"I'll round up some other witnesses. But first I want you to come to my office tomorrow morning, Ike. My secretary will be there; give her a statement."

"Statement?"

"Everything that happened from the time you got to the stadium till the last thing you can remember before you passed out."

"No, no. I ain't giving a statement to nobody. I don't need you or the NAACP or Martin Luther King or SNCC or anybody else. This is strictly my business."

"What do you mean, 'strictly your business'? What do you intend to do?"

"That's for me to know, and for you to find out."

"Ike, there's more than you involved in this thing. There's Cable, who was pushed down the steps, and Mrs. Tucker Stribling. The children, of course. Thank God none of them was hurt. But I can't make a decent case unless you are willing to press charges."

"This is between me and Buford Leggitt. He's the one who did this to me, and he's the one who's going to pay."

At that moment Reverend Cable came back. He had a shirt, some socks, a pair of trousers, and a pair of old bedroom slippers. "They want to talk to you,

Ike, take some pictures. I said it would be all right."

"I got nothing to say to them people. This is a private affair."

Reverend Cable looked at Daddy then shook his head. "All right, everybody, Doc, McIllister, that's enough. Let's leave him alone, give him a chance to get into his clothes."

"Better take a warm bath soon as you get home, put Epsom salts in the water, and get Stone to rub your back with Baume Bengué, or Sloan's liniment, if you got some."

"I don't need Stone or anybody else to rub my back or do anything else for me. Now leave me alone." Daddy slowly got to his feet, steadying himself against the back of the chair until he could stand up straight. Then he started to get into the shirt and pants that Reverend Cable had brought.

"I've got the pictures, but I still need a statement. Take your time. I know exactly how you feel," said Mr. Mac.

"Come by my office in a couple of days," Doc Wheeler said, finally lighting up a cigar, "and I'll change the bandages."

They left and Daddy continued trying to dress himself; both the shirt and the pants were a little tight, but they would do. Reverend Cable went behind his desk, sat down, and pressed a button on his phone. "Mrs. Rhettis, tell the press people that Mr. Stone doesn't care to make a statement. That will be all." He hung up and slumped down in his chair. "Sometimes I understand you, Ike, and sometimes I don't. We need to talk."

"Nothing to talk about. Give me what's mine, so I can get out of here. I got some business to attend to."

"Ike, you're mad, you're angry, you've been mistreated, and you ain't afraid to die. Everybody knows that. And after what happened to you at the rally nobody can blame you for feeling the way you feel. But feelings aren't all you got here to deal with. You got your son."

"Oh, I intend to deal with my son. You better believe it. As soon as I get him home, I'll deal with him."

"Ike, I'm asking you—no, I'm begging you, to do me a personal favor. I want you to leave your pistol here with me for a while, till things cool down. Till you've had time to think of the consequences."

"I know the consequences, and I hope Buford Leggitt knows them as well. I want my property."

"Revenge on the white man. That's all you can think about?"

"Buford Leggitt, and all his gang, brave upholders of the law, with their dogs and their water hoses and their night sticks—just for whipping heads. But so what, it's only niggers. . . . And whoever it was planted those bombs and killed Carole and Mollie Mae, and shot Medgar Evers in the back—don't worry, white folks, we love you. All we're going to do is hold hands, march, and sing 'We Shall Overcome.' Right? Well, not me, not Isaac Stone. Isaac Stone is a man."

"Yes, but just one man, Ike, with everything they got lined up against you. No matter how many Buford Leggitts you put away, they got the numbers, they got the hardware, and in the end you'll come out dead!"

"That may be true, but at least I'll die like a man! Give me my pistol."

"Seems like what happened to us in Korea don't mean a thing."

"I am not responsible for what happened in Korea. That was war."

"Oh? . . . You and me and Suggs and Burley and Mosh, we didn't kill that woman and her baby. That was war."

"Cable!" Daddy made a move, but stopped himself. If I hadn't been standing there I think he would have hit Reverend Cable. Instead, he grabbed my arm and pushed me toward the door. "Wait outside."

"No, Ike, let him stay . . . hear the story of what we did that night from your lips . . . find out what's driving you crazy."

"You hear me what I'm telling you, boy? I said wait outside!" He opened the door, pushed me through, and slammed it shut behind me. And then I heard them arguing loud and angry.

I know it's impolite to listen while grown-ups talk,

so I moved away from the door. But they kept talking so loud I couldn't help hearing what they said, even if I couldn't understand it. I walked all the way down to the rec room, but nobody was there. So I came half way back and sat down on a bench against the wall and waited. Finally, the door burst open, and Reverend Cable came out, followed by Daddy, who had to move slower but was determined not to be left behind. He was carrying the pistol in his hand.

"Well, Ike, you got what you came for. You got your God, and I got mine. So go. Go in peace, but go. Go. Go. And good riddance!"

"I'm going all right, and this time for good. I never intend to set foot in Holy Oak Baptist again!"

"Oh, you'll be back all right. After you settle things with Buford, and whoever else you got to kill. You will be back, feet first—six men to carry you, with an American flag draped across your coffin. And I will preach the funeral and tell everybody what a brave killer you were, not only in Korea, but here also. You will be buried out at Hillside, with a sixteen gun salute, right next to Lucy. So you can explain to her how—in spite of the oath you swore upon her deathbed—you managed to leave your fourteen-year-old-son—your only child—an orphan in this world. Go, and may God forgive you!"

Reverend Cable left. Daddy looked at me as if he hated me, the fire still burning in his eyes. And then he walked out of Holy Oak as if nothing was ailing his body—straight on out to the parking lot. But when he started to climb into the pickup, a sudden pain must have caught him in his side. It almost doubled him over and scared me half to death.

"Daddy, Daddy, you want me to help you?" I reached my hand out to him, but Daddy slapped it away.

"Shut up, boy, you just shut right up." He stood there, baring his teeth, sucking his breath, and sweating, until he was able to get in by himself. I climbed in too. Then he took the pistol and put it into the glove compartment. "The worst thing that ever happened to me in my whole life was having you for a son!"

Mama Lucy always said never to feel sorry for yourself, and I tried hard not to. I certainly didn't mean to be pitiful, and sad, as I lay on the bed way into the night thinking about it, and crying to myself. I guess I didn't do so well, or maybe I didn't try hard enough. I kept hearing him, seeing the way he looked as he said it, over and over and over: "The worst thing ever happened to me in my whole life was having you for a son." His disgusted voice was coming after me from far far away and deep into my dreaming.

And I was dreaming—but I don't remember about what. Later that night, in the pitch dark, Daddy came into the room and shook me awake. He told me not to go to school that morning, but to stay home and start packing. He and I were on our way to California.

Mr. McIllister had seen us through the big front window of his office and rose to meet us at the door. The place was filled with old, musty leather furniture, a hat rack, and a big picture of Booker T. Washington and a large calendar over the desk, which was old-fashioned too. Mr. Mac had graduated from Tuskegee Institute the year that Booker T. Washington had died. And every February at Negro History Week Mr. Mac came to Stedman to speak about it.

"Did you see Mrs. Tucker Stribling? She just left . . . came in and made her statement. Only trouble is, she's got a case, all right, but not really the kind we need. With you it's a different matter. Ike, you and Stone draw up a chair. Peggy has gone to the bank, but she'll be right back. I don't want to keep you waiting, but I am anxious to get that statement."

"I didn't come here to make a statement. I come here to put my house on the market. We're going to California."

"California? . . . Well, this is a surprise. You of all people. Last thing I ever expected in this world was to see Big Stone and Little Stone turning tail and running."

"If I stay here, I'm liable to kill somebody, or somebody is going to kill me. Don't make me much difference one way or the other. But I got the boy to think about too. Best thing for me is to get out of here as soon as I can."

Mr. Mac sat back down and fiddled with some papers on his desk. His chair was the kind that could spin around, and it creaked when he turned or leaned back. He always wore a clean white shirt, with a black tie like a shoelace around his neck, and nobody ever remembers seeing him without his coat on.

"Not a good time to sell, I'm afraid, real estate is way down. Might not find a buyer for six months, even a year."

"I don't care how long it takes. Here's the deed. I still owe some on the taxes. I'd like to get the money out of it as soon as possible; but I'd be willing to take back a second mortgage if I had to."

"It's a good house, Ike. You built it for your wife. I can't possibly get the kind of money it's really worth, but—"

"Then get what you can. Stone and I are leaving the first of the month. I'll write from California and give you my address."

"How you-all planning to travel? . . . by train?

"No train. We're putting everything we can into the pickup, then driving out."

"This town will hate to see the two of you go. Tell me, Ike, what do you know about California?"

"Enough to know it ain't like Alabama."

"I know it's a long ways away. And look, I'm not

sure as I blame you. Twelve years I was president of the NAACP, and many's the time I felt the same way you do, especially about Alabama: a mean and ugly season for a black man. Holy hell, that's what it was, with no plans ever to change. Why not just pack up my things and run away? But then, Rosa Parks came along and there was the bus boycott in Montgomery and Martin Luther King. That put civil rights right up there at the top of the evening news. I know it's rough, but now it's different. Now, we got the law on our side; public opinion all over this country is on our side; the Constitution of the United States of America is on our side. It's only a matter of time."

"It's more than a matter of time. I've got to get out of this town, now. That's all there is to it."

"The more you run, Ike Stone, the faster you get to what it is you're running from."

"I didn't come here for nobody to preach at me, Mr. Mac."

"I know that, Ike, but I just think you ought to reconsider. Television has put the spotlight on these people. The whole world is watching everything they do. All we got to do is to keep up the pressure—like that children's march—people all over the country are still talking about it— like Mrs. Tucker Stribling. She insists on suing the city, but with you we could go into Federal Court and— Here comes Peggy now. Just let her get her pad. All we need is that statement."

"Look, Mr. Mac there's a million things I got to do

between now and the first of the month, and you're not the only real estate agent in this town. If you don't want my business, I'll go somewhere else—like Mrs. Ellis, maybe."

"All right, Ike, keep your seat. Everybody knows how stubborn you can be, once you make up your mind to it. But what you're about to do is more serious than you think. What we're doing here is not just for us, it's for our children. It's for Stone here, your son. He's right in the middle of the school year. Have you thought about what taking him out of school in the middle of the semester, setting him down in a place where neither of you have ever been before, is going to do to your son?"

"My son? This boy is lucky I ain't broke his neck!" And with that he got up and started out.

Mr. McIllister followed us to the door, wiping his face with his handkerchief. "For God's sake, don't be so touchy. You want your house on the market, all right, all right, I'll do it."

10

Next Sunday I got up early and put on my white suit. But Ike stopped me while I was still in the bathroom.

"Where do you think you're going?"

"Mrs. Rhettis called from the church. The Young People's Bible Class is giving me a scroll, and there's a reception downstairs. Big Mother has baked me a cake ... a chance to say good-bye to my friends. So I thought maybe—"

"I don't care what you thought. I told Cable, and now I'm telling you: No more church, no more Holy Oak, and that's final."

"Yes, sir, but I thought you were only talking about yourself."

"No. I meant you too. No more Holy Oak Baptist Church, not ever."

I heard myself repeating the words. Not ever; thinking for the first time exactly what it meant. My church, and the people in it, as close to me as flesh and blood and bones—all that was gone. And what would I ever do without Reverend Cable? PeeWee said that Malcolm X was a gangster; Dorasthena said he was as great as Dr. King. Everybody looked at me; but I didn't exactly know what to say, so I was going to ask Reverend Cable about it. But it didn't matter now. Somebody else would soon be president of the Young People's Bible Class and Junior Assistant Pastor. I'd miss that most of all.

I reminded Daddy that this was the day we were supposed to pay Mrs. Ellis, and that maybe we should give her something extra to keep Mama Lucy's grave clean, and put some flowers on it from time to time. That made him stop and think a minute. "How much do we owe that nosy woman?"

"I don't know, exactly. It's been about three months since we last paid her."

"Okay. Get her on the phone. Find out what it is, tell her I'll send her a money order back from California."

I waited until I was sure she was back from church and then I called her and went to see her.

"This is the Lord's day, Stone, and I don't feel like

doing business in such a cold, hard-hearted fashion. And anyway, you and your father are my most reliable customers, so what's the rush, eh?"

"The rush is, we're leaving for California the first of the month."

"Oh, I know, Dorasthena told me you all had to sell your house. But, no, I still don't believe it."

"Daddy turned it over to Mr. Mac for him to sell."

"To Mr. Mac? But Mr. Mac is old, and he's too slow. Why didn't your father turn it over to me? Haven't I treated you fairly ever since I've been here? Haven't I? How much is your father asking?"

"I don't know, I didn't ask him."

"It's a good house, a beautiful house, and I have got to find me a better place than this. But I still don't believe it. What would this town be like without you and your father, the best cabinetmaker we have? He can't do that to us. He can't take you away from us. I won't let him. I'll tell you what. When is your father home? I must drive over there and talk to him. Plead with that man, beg him not to go."

"He working on a big housing project down in Columbiana every day. There's so many other things he got to do before we leave. He's very busy."

"I don't care how busy he is. I'll miss him. I'll miss you too. You tell him I must see him. I will not let him just move away like that. It's indecent. You tell him I said it's indecent."

"I'll tell him, ma'm. But he is awfully busy."

"And you come by here tomorrow, when he's gone, and I'll take you shopping. I'll buy you a suit, some shoes, and some decent clothes. You can't go to California looking like this. People out there would laugh at you."

"Yes, Ma'm. But I don't think my father would like that."

"Your father won't have to know. We won't tell him a thing. Tomorrow, then?"

"I haven't got any money, Mrs. Ellis."

"Did I say one thing to you about money? Didn't I say you're like a son to me? What do you think your mother would say if I let you go to California looking like a little bum, and she a seamstress—the best, the most fastidious I have ever seen? She knew clothes, your mother did, one of the best dressed women in this city. By the way, those fine dresses that I've been trying to get that father of yours to sell to me—you still have them?"

"Yes, Ma'm. All her clothes are stilling hanging in the closet."

"Surely you are not taking them to California with you. I mean what would you do with Lucy's dresses out there?"

"I don't know, ma'm. We haven't started packing them yet."

"You tell your Daddy I'm perfectly willing to forget

everything he owes me, if he'll let me have a few of Lucy's dresses. Will you tell him that for me? Don't you think that's fair?'"

Next morning, very early, while I was fixing his breakfast, I told my father about Mrs. Ellis, and the dresses in Mama Lucy's closet. He got mad—angry—as I knew he would.

"Lucy's dresses! Over my dead body. Put everything that belongs to your mother, especially her dresses, into the trunk."

"The trunk is too small—it's already full."

"Well, empty it then. Take everything out except your mother's stuff . . . her shoes, her hats, her dresses, her petticoats, her stockings, her underwear, her needles and thread, and her sewing machine."

"The first thing I tried was the sewing machine. It's too big."

"I told you to wrap it up in a quilt, or maybe a blanket, and tie it tight with some rope. Everything that belonged to Lucy, from her thimble to her umbrella, we take. Is that clear?" He was gulping down his coffee and moving toward the door.

It wasn't clear, none of it was. I didn't see how we were going to pack all our stuff onto the back of the pickup and haul it all the way to California. But Daddy was still mad at me about the pistol. So I didn't ask him anything, or tell him anything he might not want to hear. I was afraid to. I didn't tell him about Mr. Maples, the undertaker, who called to ask if Daddy wanted to sell his plot over at the cemetery. "Is Ike planning to be shipped back here to be buried beside his wife, or is he going to stay in California?"

"But Daddy, even with the trunk, the two suitcases, and the cardboard boxes, it still won't be enough to hold what we got in this house."

"I'm bringing some more boxes home and plenty of rope. What we don't take we'll leave in storage. Mr. Mac can send it when he sells the house."

The phone rang. I picked it up. It was Professor Duckett. Daddy told me to take a message, then drove on off.

"Daddy just left, but he told me to take a message, sir."

"You haven't been excused from classes yet, so why aren't you at school today?"

"It's only a few more days before we leave, and there's still a lot to do. So Daddy thought I ought to stay home today and finish up the packing, but I'll be there tomorrow, sir."

"Be sure you do, Stone, and tell your father even if he hasn't returned my call you are still enrolled in Stedman. I still insist on seeing the two of you in person here in my office before you leave this jurisdiction, you understand me?"

"Yes, sir. I'll tell him as soon as he gets back from Columbiana."

"Columbiana?"

"He's working on a housing project over there."

"Tell him if he doesn't, I fully intend to hold back your transcript, not send your records at all, and no school in California, or anywhere else, will accept you without those records over my signature. Be sure to tell him that, you understand me?"

"Yes, sir. I'll be sure to tell him."

"Look, Stone, I'm sorry." He sighed into the phone like he was apologizing. "I don't want to seem too hard, but, well, I'm worried. You see, there are some good schools out on the West Coast, but none of 'em's black. You've got to go to Morehouse, especially if you're planning to be anything at all like Martin Luther King. Now there's got to be some way we can work this whole thing out—there's got to. Please, Stone, tell Ike to call me, will you?"

"Yes, sir, but would you please excuse me, sir? Someone's knocking on the door, and I've got to go. Excuse me." I hung up and went to the door. It was Mrs. Rhettis, the church secretary, and Big Mother, who came in behind her carrying two large shopping bags filled to the brim.

"I haven't set foot in this house since the wake. You and Ike have certainly kept it clean. Lucy would be so pleased." Mrs. Rhettis was almost whispering as she moved slowly into the living room, looking all around her, as if she were in a church. Big Mother headed straight back for the kitchen: "I brought you some of the cake we had for you at church, and also some fried chicken and fish for when you out on the road. I hope there's a freezer in the refrigerator."

"And I brought the scroll and the medal for winning the oratorical contest last February at the church. And this one is from Reverend Cable." Mrs. Rhettis unwrapped a Holy Bible with my initials engraved in gold on the white leather cover. "Now show me the sewing room."

I took her through the hall and opened the door. The room was cool and dark and quiet. The old Singer sewing machine—Mama Lucy's pride and joy, so I made it my business to keep it polished—was right in front of the window, just like she left it. A dummy for fitting dresses on was standing in the corner. Mrs. Rhettis touched them both, almost as if she was scared that they might break, then went to Mama's closet. "May I?" she said, and opened the sliding door. The closet was big and long and full of Mama's dresses, some of which still had the smell of perfume. Mrs. Rhettis stood for a while, just looking, then reached in and touched some of the dresses with her finger. "What are you doing with these?"

"Daddy says to take them all and pack them in the trunk. But I don't know."

"Well, if you want me to keep some of them, at least till you get settled, and send them on . . ." She looked a minute longer, then closed the closet door, and we went out.

Big Mother was just getting back from the kitchen. "I put everything I could into the refrigerator, enough to last you and Ike all the way across the country. The rest you can eat tonight—smothered pork chops, with onions and gravy, to go with the greens and peas and rice." She sighed, her shoulders sagged. All of a sudden her voice didn't sound like a Mack truck anymore. "I'm going to miss you, boy. The whole church is too. I don't know what Reverend Cable is going to do without you."

"I'm going to miss you, too, Big Mother." She grabbed me and hugged me tight, then let me go, blowing her nose.

"This sure is a beautiful house," she said, looking around. "You tell Isaac I said so. Come on Rhettis, let's you and me get on back to the church."

I went back to class the following day, but it wasn't easy, just sitting there, waiting for the time to pass. Everybody wanted to talk, but nobody wanted to be serious. Instead they wanted to know how far Daddy and I would be from Hollywood.

When lunchtime came I met Dorasthena behind the gym under the sycamore tree—our usual place. She was spreading a napkin on the bench when I got there.

"I tried to cook some biscuits with buttermilk this morning. Some got burned."

"Oh, thanks Dorasthena, being burned don't matter."

"The rest of it I got from the store. There's boiled ham, cheese, and peanut butter, some jelly, and a piece of coconut cake. And also some milk and diet soda. I hope it's enough."

"Of course it's enough. I'm really not all that hungry." I wondered about her father, and what she would do if he hit her again. But all of that would have to be left up to Mrs. Edison and Reverend Cable now.

"Reverend Cable preached about you and Ike going away, like the Prodigal Son, to a far country. He was very good. Everybody missed you at the church. But I am not surprised your father wouldn't let you come, mean as he is."

"And I missed being there too"—letting her comments about Daddy pass.

"I've decided to go to the cemetery once a month, to see after the graves. I already started. Went all the way out there last Thursday by myself. I planted a rosebush for Mollie Mae and Carole."

"You did? . . . that's very nice."

"I found my grandmother's grave too. It was all grown over with weeds, but I pulled them up and cleaned it off. I was ashamed. It was the first time I saw it since they put her there. Course we didn't put up a stone yet, so I can't be all that sure if it's really her; but I put a flower there anyway. Would you like me to plant one for Mrs. Lucy too? A rosebush, I mean? I could look after it."

"Oh, yes, I would like that very much."

"And also, I got you a going away present. Only—"

"A present?" I said, thinking about what she must have spent on the lunch. "Dorasthena, you don't have to give me a present."

"I know I don't but I want to. It's something I want you to have to remember me by. You remember my mother's gold locket, with the chain, and her picture in it? I showed it to you once when I brought it to school. I want you to have it."

"No, Dorasthena. It's yours. It belongs to you, and anyway that's something for a girl to wear."

"You could give it to your girl, when you get one in California. I wouldn't mind. Really I wouldn't . . . only—"

The last thing in the world I wanted was something that valuable and precious—and for girls. But how could I say no? I'd get her all upset and mad at me, this being our last time together.

"Only you'll have to wait a while to get it. I had it hid like I told you. But Daddy found it, and—well, it's in the pawn shop now. But I got the ticket. And Mr. Wembley told me he'd let me pay it off a little at a time."

Pay it off with what? I asked myself. She was only a girl, and didn't even have a job. But I didn't tell her that.

"You'll have to write to me from California, let me

know where to send it. You'll have to write me a lot, Stone, I mean it. 'Cause you're my friend." Her lip was beginning to tremble.

"Yes, Dorasthena, I will. I'll write you a lot." Then we just sat there, looking at each other. Not knowing what else to say for fear that we'd be crying, and get all mushy and gloppy about everything. I found myself looking all around, saying good-bye with my eyes to everything in sight. Then I heard something, far off and way above our heads. I looked and saw way up in the sky, not a bunch, like sometimes, but a long thin line of geese, stretching across the hills, being pulled along by the leader. You could barely hear the honking, that's how high they were. And while I was looking up, she grabbed my face in both her hands—Dorasthena did—pulled me down, kissed me on the lips, and then she ran. I stood and watched until she turned the corner. I found myself wanting to cry. But, thank God, I didn't. I did have to sit down for a minute. And that's where I stayed, till PeeWee came running up.

"Hey, look at the goodies. Can I have some?" He didn't wait for an answer, just started shoving stuff into his mouth. I reached out and grabbed his hand and stopped him.

"No, PeeWee, no, you may not. And spit out what you got in your mouth. Spit it out. All of it."

PeeWee, in total surprise, opened his mouth and spat out everything in a hurry. I was sorry that I had yelled at him, but I couldn't help it. I was angry and had to take it out on somebody. He looked at me, started to say something, and changed his mind. Then he sat down, put his hands in his lap, and dropped his head.

"California," he finally said, and sounded like I had never heard before. "Boy, I sure wish I was going with you. You think your daddy would take me along too? I could find a job, take care of myself, huh?"

I didn't bother to answer, and didn't even look at him.

"Don't get angry at me, Stone." I was surprised. He'd never sounded that straight and plain before. "I know I been a pest, but well, you—and Dorasthena—are the closest thing to a family I ever had. I'm really going to be an orphan now." He took my hand in his, then let it drop. He looked at me, and there were tears in his eyes. "Good-bye, Stone." He turned to go, but I stopped him. And reached into my book bag.

"PeeWee. Remember my copy of Dr. King's I Have a Dream speech . . . the one he autographed? Here. You keep it for me."

"Could I? But Stone, I couldn't."

"You told me you wanted it, so here. Take it."

He took the three sheets of paper, folded them carefully, then put them into his pocket and shuffled off down the hall. He looked back once, and waved, and then was gone.

Saying good-bye to people your own age is tough enough—but grown-ups? You're never quite sure whether they understand, or mean what they keep on saying over and over again. It's awkward and yucky and stiff. Everybody wants to pat you on the head or say something silly. It took a long time for me to get up the courage to knock on Professor Duckett's door, then open it, and go in.

"Come in, Stone. Your father called . . . just left Doc Wheeler's, he and Mac McIllister are on their way . . . said for you to wait for them here. Come on in. Meanwhile, we've got a surprise. There's somebody here who wants to see you and say good-bye."

It was Hookie Fenster, in a wheelchair, sitting across the room. He'd lost a lot of weight. He was wearing a hospital robe and had a heavy blanket covering his lap and his leg. His father pushed him over to where I was. There was a black patch over where he had lost his eye, but I could tell that he was glad to see me. But I am not so sure I was glad to see him. There was no end to it. It had all been too much. This was one good-bye too many.

He held out his one good hand, and I thought he wanted to shake mine, but he grabbed my wrist and held on tight.

"He wants to say something to you, Stone."

"Yes, sir," I said, trying to free my wrist. But Hookie was strong and squeezed me even tighter. He looked me in the eye as hard as he could and tried to talk. What came out of his mouth was loud and singsongy—like he was gargling, or choking; but I couldn't understand a word.

"Hookie really likes you, Stone. You were always one of his favorites. He wants to go to Hollywood with you and become a movie star and win an Oscar, like Sidney Poitier. He really likes you."

Hookie heard his father and nodded his head at me as fast as he could.

All of a sudden I was ashamed of myself. He was trying the best he knew how to say he was sorry. To make up for all the unfriendly things I was still letting stand between us. What would Dr. King have said about the way I was behaving? Instead of trying to pull my hand away, I let him have it. Then I smiled at him and leaned over and hugged him. He stopped trying to talk, just sat there, holding my hand in his lap, his good eye gleaming.

Just then the door opened, and Mr. Mac came rushing in followed by Daddy, and Mrs. Edison, and somebody I didn't know. They were all talking at once like they were arguing—as if they were arguing—except Daddy, who looked around the room, worried, until he saw me, and hurried over to where I was.

"You-all ain't heard the news? Well, turn on the radio, Duckett, something awful has happened." Mr. Mac sounded scared. Mrs. Edison pressed her handkerchief hard against her mouth. "Somebody over in Dallas has shot the President!"

There was a small radio on the principal's desk and he turned it on. Everybody gathered around it except Daddy and me. The man on the radio said that somebody in a building where they kept school books had shot the President. He didn't know how serious it was, but they had rushed him to the hospital.

Others from the outside came running in until the office was almost full, with everybody crowding around trying to get closer to the radio. I wanted to get closer too, but Daddy held me back. Nobody said a word; everybody was listening to what the man on the radio was saying, over and over. He didn't seem sure of exactly what had happened and whether the President was still alive or not. Then there was a pause, and with a catch in his voice he said: "President John F. Kennedy is dead."

It was still, and it was silent. There was no sound except for Mrs. Edison trying not to cry. Then Mr. Mac said, "Oh, my God!" and turned the radio off. Professor Duckett snatched up the phone and tried to call his wife. Somebody turned the radio back on but made it lower.

Daddy stood for a while, watching what was going on. He took me by the arm and led me away. Once out in the hall, we almost ran, bumping into people going the other way. "We got to get out of this place. We got to get out of here, now. The whole world's gone crazy!"

We ran into the parking lot, jumped into his pickup,

and took off—him grinding the gears, clenching his teeth, fighting the wheel, and staring straight ahead. And me praying to the Heavenly Father that nothing got in our way.

"Where're we going to, Daddy?"

"Columbiana, to get my money." Through the streets, out onto the highway, and south as fast as we could go. I wanted him to slow down, but I was more scared of him than I was of his driving. So I sat still, clenching my fists as tight as I could. It didn't help. The radio was on, and Daddy even changed stations several times, but all you could hear was ". . . somebody has killed the President!" After a while I noticed the pickup was slowing down, until finally we got so slow everybody else was passing us. Meanwhile Daddy sat there staring straight ahead, looking strange and deeply lost in thought.

The housing project where he was working as a carpenter covered two whole city blocks. The last time he had brought me out to see it, people with hard hats— mostly white, but here and there somebody colored— were working all over, busy as bees in a beehive. Everybody busy, everybody in a hurry; but not now. Now nothing was moving. Everything had stopped, and most of the people were gone. Those still there were standing around talking and shaking their heads. Daddy showed the guard his ID and drove over to the trailer where the office was, but the door was closed. Several carpenters, who worked in Daddy's crew—

colored, of course, hired because they would work for less—were sitting around outside huddled together, although it wasn't cold.

"Why is the office locked up?"

"Ain't you heard? The President's been killed. The woman who handles the payroll left about an hour ago, but she said she was coming back. You'll have to wait like the rest of us if you want your money."

Daddy doesn't like to wait, and I almost expected him to turn right around and head back. But he didn't. We sat there and waited too. A heavy-set man who chewed tobacco was talking, mostly to himself:

"Medgar Evers in June, them two little girls in September, now, November 22, 1963, the President of the United States of America, shot down in cold blood. Ought to be something people could do so things like that couldn't happen." He looked at the ground, knowing how foolish he sounded, apologizing.

A long wait, then someone else spoke up. "If they did that to the President, and him a white man, what you reckon they'd do to us?" The question sat there, quivering and unanswered—something dark and scary at the back of a black man's mind.

"It takes more than one man to kill a president. It takes a whole country—a country that would rather die than set the black man free. Don't you think so, Ike?" the fat man asked.

Daddy didn't move, didn't say a word; I wasn't sure if anybody expected him to.

"Yeah, whoever did it, did it to represent what the white folks really think." This from a man with smooth black skin and white whiskers. "They seen Kennedy as being on the side of the Negro, and that was too much. That's what I think."

The fat man turned his head and spat, and spoke again: "Kennedy, he's not just a man, he's the President, he represents the whole country. That's why I say it takes more than just one somebody to kill the President. 'Cause it's almost the same as if you were trying to kill the country."

"See, there? That's how lies get started. It says on the radio one man, one somebody. What makes you think anybody else was connected?" This from a big, tall man with wide shoulders, who spoke and moved a little aside from the rest.

The fat man wouldn't give up. "Maybe only one somebody did pull the trigger. Maybe there was a few other fellow murderers, egging him on, giving him advice if not assistance; but that's not what I mean . . . that's not enough to kill a president. That's something it takes the whole country to do. Everybody guilty, some of us before the fact, and some of us after."

Another man took exception. "What you mean *us*? Ain't no *us* involved in this thing. This is strictly white folks. And I certainly ain't white." He laughed, but nobody else did.

"It might have started with what one man thought he was doing, but that ain't where it stops," a little, skinny man said, without taking his eyes off his whittling.

"It can't stop there." The fat man said, raising his voice a little. "You can't kill a president without the whole country being caught up in it—guilty or not guilty."

"Everybody, white folks, and black folks too, in our own way, we're all guilty. Is that what you're saying?" The man with the white beard was having as hard a time trying to figure it out as the others were.

"John Kennedy was white. God knows I don't have much truck with white folks, but more than that, he was a man, a human being, he was the President for heaven's sakes, and ain't nobody gonna put the blood of a president on my head. How about you, Isaac?" The fat man just wouldn't let Daddy alone.

Then the foreman drove up and told us the job was closed till further notice, and everybody would have to clear the premises.

Everything I heard that whole day stayed jammed up in my head and on my mind, bumping 'round and 'round until I thought it would choke me, and I was numb. I needed to talk to somebody, somebody besides the radio and the television; somebody grown up to explain to me what was going on. But as far as Isaac Stone, my own father, was concerned, I might as well not even have been alive. He wasn't talking. At least not to me.

After dinner we sat down in the living room to watch television. Daddy kept changing from one channel to another but all he could get was the same thing. One time a reporter was on talking to Dr. King, who was saying something about all of us being caught in a "web of mutuality." I didn't know exactly what that meant but it sounded impressive. I wanted to talk to Daddy, ask him about it, but I didn't get the chance. He snorted like an angry bull, turned off the television, and went out, got into his pickup, and left without a word.

I wanted to hear the rest of what Dr. King was saying on television, but I didn't know if I should turn it on again without Daddy's permission. Before I could make up my mind, I fell asleep in the chair.

It was already daylight when Daddy came in, shook me, woke me up, and stood for a moment, not smiling exactly, but so relaxed—such a big change in his eyes. And the way he looked, I could tell something very important must have happened.

"Son." He smiled at me and put his hand on my face—the first time he touched me since about the pistol. "I shouldn't have left you alone all night like that, and I'm sorry. I'm very sorry." He pulled me up out the chair and stood with his hands on my shoulders, looking down at me for the longest time. And then he hugged me and squeezed me till it hurt. I was too surprised and delighted to say anything. He tickled my chin, and I laughed, and he laughed and let me go. He plopped into a chair and kept on talking.

"They shot the President, and that just about drove me crazy. I was so full and scrambling in my mind, I thought my head would bust, that I was losing control. I had to get out, get away from everybody, even you. I drove for a while, don't know how long, but McIllister is right: the more you run, the faster you get to what it is you running from. I wound up inside the cemetery, sitting on the grass, next to Lucy, thinking thoughts that only a black could think—holding on for dear life. I remember being angry, mad as hell, at Lucy for dying and leaving us. So dizzy, I tried to stand up and couldn't; like an elephant trapped in quicksand with no bottom—the more you struggle, the more you can't get out.

"Then all of a sudden out of nowhere it hit me like a flash of lightning. And I saw it, Stone, saw it as plain as day, right there in front of my mind: I didn't want to go to California. 'Ain't got no business in California,' saying to myself. 'My place is here with my son and my wife and my people, God bless us all, and this house I built for you and that woman out there in the grave, right here in Alabama.' Peace, son, in great big waves like the ocean sweeping me off my feet. It felt so good I wanted to jump up and down and tell everybody. The whole wide world was different, and I was too, and all of a sudden, never so hungry in my life. You think you could fix us some breakfast?"

This time it was me—it was I—that hugged him. And I was crying and laughing at the same time. "You get washed up, Daddy, this won't take me long." I ran to the kitchen, lit the stove, put on some grits, started my coffee, put some country sausage meat into the skillet, then set the table. I always wait till he's sitting at the table before I scramble my eggs. I put out the butter, the milk, and the last jar of watermelon rind preserve that Mama Lucy had left us, started my toast, and then called him; but he didn't come. I thought maybe he was taking a shower, so I called him again, louder this time. No answer, so I went back to his room and found him lying across the bed fast asleep.

It was way after noon before he waked. And then we sat down at the table and we ate—I mean we cleaned the plates, and burped and laughed and joked.

"Hurry it up," he said, after we had finished. "Get your hat, and bring a jacket—we got a trip to make." He went out to the garage and I could hear him puttering around while I piled the dishes into the sink. I got my hat and went into the living room and turned on the television and watched for a minute. I saw Vice-President Lyndon Johnson, standing on the plane, taking the oath of office. Then they showed pictures of people from all over the world, telling how sad they felt or what they were doing at the time the President was shot.

"Somebody you don't know," Daddy had come back in so quietly I hadn't heard him, "never even heard of, picks up a rifle, and makes you a murderer too. Let's go. We got to get to the lake before the sun goes down." I noticed he was carrying the big basket he uses for tackle, but he didn't have a pole, and that was strange. But I was too full of joy and fun and being glad to start asking questions. He was my daddy, and my daddy wasn't angry at me anymore, and that was enough. I asked if maybe I should fix us some sandwiches. He said he was sure he couldn't eat another mouthful until next week. We laughed and got into the pickup and started for the lake. It was more than an hour's drive, but this time Daddy didn't seem in a hurry, which made it nice.

"You know, son, fourteen years ago, when you were being born I wasn't here. I was in the Army, killing people for a living. In Korea. My country drafted me. My country taught me. My country sent me. So what did they expect me to do—go over there and say I come in peace? I was a soldier . . . a darn good soldier, and it wasn't me that did it, it was them—the Army. The President of the United States, Harry S Truman, he gave the orders. Whatever happened over there, it wasn't my fault. I was just following orders. Or so I have been thinking all this time. But now, I'm not so sure. That's why I'm going to the lake, and I want you to go with me."

We had left the city by then and turned off the highway and were moving along a winding country road with a lot of tall, straight pine trees on both sides. The sun was still high, the shadows from the trees still short, but not for long. It was about three o'clock, and there was a long trail of dust rising up behind us.

Mr. Peterson was at the lake, renting boats as usual; but business was slow. "They killed the President, so a lot of people are just staying home, I reckon," he said, "watching it on television. I got a set myself, right here in my shack, had it on all night. It sure is a spectacle."

The boat we got this time was better than before, it didn't leak. "Here, you carry this, and I'll row." Daddy handed me the fishing basket and picked up the oars. The sky was still bright, but the sun was moving faster to the west and would soon be heading down.

It was a little chilly as we headed out. Daddy had on a kind of a jersey and a rough old sweater he sometimes worked in. I had on a pair of overalls over my clothes. He rowed for a long time without talking. Then he stopped and sat there looking sad and distant, thinking God knows what for the longest time. Then he sighed and started rowing again.

In the middle of the lake he stopped again, shipped the oars, and took the basket and opened it. His voice was calm and easy—his look serene and peaceful. Out came the pistol, polished, oiled, blue and shiny; but he began, with his long black nimble fingers, softly to rub the gleaming metal anyway, using the oily towel he had wrapped it in. And as he rubbed he talked.

"There were four of us that night, out on patrol. My finger was on the trigger of my rifle, because I was point man, and I was scared. And then, from a clump of bushes right up ahead, barely visible in the moonlight, I heard a noise and started shooting. I started first, then everybody jumped in, throwing everything we had into those bushes. We stopped and waited and listened. Nothing. Still as the grave. And quiet. We should have run, gotten out of there. The Koreans, hearing all that ruckus, were sure to send a patrol to investigate. But me and Cable, we stayed behind, and using our lights—which was strictly against regulations—we looked. It wasn't a soldier. It was a woman we had shot, her baby still clutched in her arms, a bloody mess, impossible to tell the two apart. Blood, bones, hair, bowels, teeth, one eye—the mother's still looking, but no life . . . Raw heart still beating in the baby's rib cage."

He had taken six bullets while he talked, and put them, one by one, into the chamber. He wrapped the pistol carefully in waxed paper and then in brown paper, two or three times over, then took some good, stout fishing twine from the basket and wrapped it around several times. Then, letting out the string a little at a time, he lowered the little package into the water.

"Cable threw his rifle away; wouldn't touch it, even on direct orders from the company commander. They sent him home; he got to be a preacher. Suggs eventually went crazy. Burley got to be a drunk, and Mosh killed himself. Everybody paid his dues but me."

Down it went—the package, little by little, giving off lots of bubbles for a while, then getting slower and slower, until finally, they stopped. He sighed and sat there looking at where he had dropped the string.

"I don't know, maybe it did take a whole country and a government to do it, but in the end, it wasn't the captain, or the sergeant, or the President of the United States, got me to pull that trigger—it was me."

The hills beyond were so covered now with shadows, it was hard to tell the water from the woods. "Poor woman, trying, as a mother will, to save her child. As God is my judge, I'm sorry I took your life. And hope that, maybe somehow, you can find it in your heart to forgive me for what I done."

By now, the sun was gone, and dark was coming faster and faster. Mosquitoes buzzed and bit me. The fireflies came out, the sound of the crickets got louder, and one by one, the bullfrogs started in too. I couldn't see his face, or whether there were any tears in his eyes; but I knew my daddy was crying. So I picked up the oars and started rowing back.

11

Daddy had changed, which means everything between him and me had changed too. There were a lot of things we needed to talk about, but somehow he got to be even quieter than before, and knowing him, I realized I'd have to wait. One thing he did say one morning before he left for Columbiana: "I'm glad we don't have to worry about going to California anymore." And that was enough for me.

The week after Thanksgiving we had another visit from Mutts Malone, who was Assistant Coach at Morehouse, and Professor Duckett asked me to be the host and show him around. Dorasthena called me a coward, and said I ought to tell Mutts that I was not going to be a football player, but a preacher like Dr. King, but I didn't get around to it.

Christmas was on the way, and we wanted it to be different, to honor the memory of Mollie Mae and Carole, and Mrs. Edison said that maybe the best way would be if nobody would buy presents from any of the stores, but if each of us would make somebody a gift with our own hands. That way it would be more spiritual and not so commercial. Dorasthena said we ought to ask everybody in Holy Oak to do the same thing and give the money we saved to Dr. King. I wanted to talk to Daddy about all of this, but he seemed all tied up with something on his mind that he wasn't ready to talk about.

The second Sunday in December Daddy and I drove to Holy Oak as we had done so many times before. This was Martin Luther King, Jr., day, and to tell the truth I was hoping that, this time, Daddy would come with me into the service, but he didn't. Instead he sat out in the pickup, no different from what he had been doing ever since Mama Lucy died.

Inside the place was packed again, and this time, so much so, that we in the Young People's Bible Class gave up our seats to the visitors and stood around the wall. This was the first time Martin Luther King, Jr., was to preach the eleven o'clock sermon in more than a year. And that meant many more people than the seats could handle.

Dr. King asked the whole congregation to join him and the choir and sing an old Negro spiritual which was a favorite of his, and had been since his childhood. Everybody stood. Holy Oak has always been known for good singing, but this time was the best I ever heard.

> "Going to lay down my sword and shield,
>   Down by the riverside,
>   Down by the riverside,
>   Down by the riverside.
> Going to lay down my sword and shield
>   Down by the riverside, and
> Study war no more.
>
>   Ain't going to study war no more,
>   Ain't going to study war no more,
>   Ain't going to study war no more,
>   I ain't going to study war no more,
>   Ain't going to study war no more,
>   Ain't going to study war no more."

When the song was over, a whisper of excitement, the rattling of paper, and the rustle of clothes ran through the crowd like electricity. Then everybody settled down to hear what Dr. King would have to say.

First he thanked Reverend Cable, the Holy Oak congregation, and the good people of our fair city for making him feel so welcome and right at home. Next he talked about the new marches and demonstrations—"bigger and better than ever"—and the new voter registration drives which were being planned, and which would continue until "justice rolls down like waters and righteousness like a mighty stream . . . until segregation and Jim Crow come tumbling down like the Walls of Jericho."

Daddy was out in the truck; they had the loudspeakers on so I knew he could hear everything. But Dr. King is something to see as well as hear: his flashing eyes, the way his head reared back, with his mouth opened wide, like a trumpet, his hands moving like wings. Daddy was missing the best half of it.

"It is with heavy hearts that we approach the season dedicated to the birth of the Prince of Peace, knowing full well that this has been one of the bloodiest, most violent years in American history, short of war. Medgar Evers in Jackson, Mississippi; two beautiful young children, right here in Holy Oak; and less than a month ago, our President, John F. Kennedy. I haven't met the new President yet, and time alone will tell whether he is a good man or not, but certainly no one is more deserving of our prayers and good wishes than Lyndon B. Johnson."

Everybody in the church said something nice about the new President.

"But no matter the dark and violent coloration of these times I still can say I am mighty glad to be here with you this morning, glad because it gives me a chance to meet the brave young people of this city."

With that he looked every one of us in the face: he even pointed at us. ". . . and to express to them the deep, deep debt of gratitude we owe our children for having set such a magnificent example, not only for grown-ups, but also for the nation and the world. To thank them from the bottom of my heart for the courage, determination, and the fiery but stubborn commitment to nonviolence as a way of struggle in the children's march. Let the church say amen."

Everybody said amen. Dr. King paused awhile, to give the congregation time to catch its breath, to shift our feet, and move our eyes around and look at each other before we settled down again. I noticed—when Dr. King started again—a little change in his voice, a looser rhythm and a lower tone. More like good, plain talk than preaching. But just as strong and powerful and urgent.

"The Apostle Paul said in his letter to the Corinthians: 'If the trumpet give an uncertain sound, who shall prepare himself for battle?'"

Everybody knew this passage from the Bible, so most of us took the words right out of his mouth and finished it before he did. We do that all the time at Holy Oak Baptist, helping the speaker, whoever he is, to preach his sermon, especially if he is good and knows how to lead us. And nobody can beat Dr. King.

"This trumpet blast, this call to arms, sounded by these valiant boys and girls was in no ways uncertain.

Rather, as in the majestic words of Julia Ward Howe, 'They have sounded forth a trumpet that shall never call retreat!' And we too must follow their example. We must prepare ourselves to see that the battle continues. A battle all the more moral because it is nonviolent, all the more glorious because you can only fight it with love. A victory all the more certain, because God is always on the side of the righteous."

These words: big, wonderful, and magnificent . . . swashing through the congregation like thunder and lightning. Yet they were soft and warm and soothing also; the church was lit with its own inward summer, the people like an ocean rising and falling in a wave of peace, lifted above ourselves by what we heard.

When service was over everybody crowded around Dr. King, wanting to touch him and shake his hand and tell him how much they were praying for him. PeeWee wriggled his way through the crowd and got to me: "I just saw your father," he shouted, "at the back of the church, sitting in the very last row."

At first I thought he was kidding; but he wouldn't dare. I tried to restrain myself. After all, though service was over, we were still in the sanctuary, trying to help Dr. King make his way downstairs. But this was too much.

"Last row? Okay, PeeWee, you stay here and help. Keep the people moving. I'll get Daddy and meet you all downstairs."

I made my way against the crowd toward the rear of the church. I wanted more than anything for Daddy to meet Dr. King, face-to-face, to shake hands with him. Then he would understand. But when I got there the back row was empty, and Daddy was gone.

I found him outside, sitting in the pickup. "I was sitting here," he said, "listening to Dr. King on the speaker, when I saw the Edlee brothers riding by in their truck. They went on up the street, then turned around and drove back by going the other way. They weren't loud or making any noise or anything like that. But the whole thing was creepy, and I didn't like it. I didn't exactly know what to do, so I decided that maybe I'd better come on inside. And so I did."

"You heard the speech. You saw him?"

"Yes."

"And did you like it?"

He thought for a moment. "Yes. I liked it." And that was all he would say.

Next day Daddy was waiting to pick me up after school as usual. "I brought your toolbox," he said. I hadn't the slightest idea of what that was supposed to mean.

"You did . . . but why, Daddy?"

"I understand," he explained, "they're planning to start rebuilding over at Holy Oak. I thought you and I might go over there and maybe give them a hand."

It was about 4:00 P.M. when we pulled into the parking lot at Holy Oak Baptist. Mrs. Tucker Stribling's old Rolls-Royce was standing in Daddy's usual spot, so he parked right next to it. Daddy got out and took his toolbox from the back. "You bring the rest of the stuff." Reverend Cable met us at the door. He didn't seem surprised.

"Well, first I saw you come in yesterday and stand up in the back. Now the very next day you're here again."

"Yeah. Little Stone and I thought maybe we'd come over and give you a hand. We brought our tools."

"Well, we certainly need all the help we can get. But more than that, I hope this means that you are coming back to us, Isaac, back for good." Daddy took time to think his thought before he said it.

"Yes, it does, Josh. Back for good—if you will have me." They stood for a moment, just looking at each other. Then Reverend Cable stuck out his hand, and Daddy grabbed it. There was a look between the two that almost made me cry.

"Well, well, well—just like the Prodigal Son, huh? Welcome home, Isaac, old friend, welcome home."

Then they hugged each other and laughed a little.

"Yep . . . yep. So where is the fatted calf?"

"Big Mother's in the kitchen right now, and you know her. You get to eat only after you finish your labor." He grabbed Daddy by the arm and the two of them started downstairs. With me trailing along behind.

"You know, Isaac, except for yesterday, this is the first time you set your foot in Holy Oak Baptist since Lucy died. She would be so proud."

"Yeah. I think she would."

"This is your church, you know, yours, and hers. The two of you got married here."

"I'm back, Josh, but before we get too far" — Daddy stopped and turned to Reverend Cable — "I need to talk to you, I need to talk to you, bad. The Edlee brothers are still out there, and they mean business. The more I try to make sense about this nonviolent thing, the more confused I get. You got to talk to me, Cable, explain this thing better than you've done up till now."

"I'll do better than that. I'll introduce you to the man who is an expert, who knows all of the answers. Hey Martin . . ." The man he was talking to had his back to us. His coat was off, and his shirt sleeves were rolled up — it was Dr. King! He was bending over a pile of eight-foot-long two by two's. He held a hammer in his hand, but he didn't seem to know what to do with it. He straightened and looked around and I thought — what a wonderful smile.

"Jesus of Nazareth was a carpenter," Reverend Cable said, laughing. "I sure hope he was better at it than you." Dr. King laughed also, and said he hoped so too. "Martin, this is Isaac Stone Senior, father of Isaac Stone Junior, president of the Young People's Bible Class. Big Stone and Little Stone, we call them sometimes. Big Stone needs somebody to explain to him about nonviolence and to do it in a hurry."

"Well, I hope I'm better at that than I am with this hammer. Glad to meet you, Brother Stone." Dr. King smiled, and held out his hand. Daddy hesitated for a moment, and then he took it.

"Big Mother's fixing lunch in the kitchen," Reverend Cable said. "You two can talk in there. I have some business to take care of with Mrs. Tucker Stribling, and then I'll join you. Stone" — he turned to me — "the rest of the kids are rehearsing in the rec room."

"Yes, sir." I'd already heard the music, Pearlicia playing 'We Shall Overcome.' Dorasthena met me at the door and snatched me inside. Something was up. She had that look on her face. The room was full. Reverend Cable had asked us to put together a program in honor of Dr. King, who was going to talk to the workshop in creative nonviolence before he left. PeeWee was at the lectern reading aloud.

"I say to you, my friends, that in spite of the difficulties and frustrations of the moment, I still have a dream."

Dorasthena was furious. "See? See what you've done? Donald Duck could do it better than that."

"What do you mean, see what I have done?"

"He said you gave him the speech, that you wanted him to recite it for Dr. King."

"I did give it to him, but only as a going away

present. I didn't say anything about him reciting it."

"Well, there he is, doing it. Is that how you want Dr. King to hear his speech being delivered?"

PeeWee was pumping his hands and rolling his eyes— ". . . that one day the state of Alabama, whose governor's lips are presently dripping with the words of . . .of . . . interposition and . . . and nullification. . ."

Dorasthena was right—PeeWee was awful, and now he was beginning to stumble over the words.

"Don't just stand there like an idiot. Do something."

Do something. That was just like Dorasthena. Do what? She acted like—she acted as if being president of the class made me some kind of dictator or something. PeeWee had as much right to recite the speech as I had. But maybe I could help him, show him how.

I walked toward the front of the room. PeeWee saw me coming, and his eyes lit. He ran to meet me and put the speech in my hand. "Boy, am I glad to see you." Then he went and sat down, grinning as usual.

I went to the lectern and turned around, and they were all there, just like old times. All my friends and classmates, looking at me and smiling. Billy Cabelle, Roscoe Malone, Morgan Heard, Thelma Dodd—and Hookie too. His father had brought him, as well as some kids from the other churches. It was almost as if I had really been away to California but now I was back home again. Dorasthena—I think she was proud of me—took a seat right next to PeeWee, and sat there, waiting. Pearlicia sat with her back to the piano. I put the speech on the lectern, I didn't need it. And then I recited what I had been practicing for a long long time, which now I knew as well as I knew my own name:

"I have a dream today . . ."